“Meredith A[illegible] nightmares that will give adventurous readers the sweetest cavities.”

- **Myriam Gurba, author of *Painting Their Portraits in Winter***

“Meredith Alling is viscously mesmerizing. She takes reality and crumbles it up tight in her hands, wringing and smashing and squeezing it to death and when she opens her hands there is a bright flash and music bursting out of everything. *Sing the Song* is incredible, it devours normal.”

- **Bud Smith, author of *F250***

“Meredith Alling’s song is one I haven’t heard before, her every sharp note a surprise. At every opportunity, Alling twists the mundane into the wild and unexpected. Her stories are born of keen observations, revealing a world I didn’t know existed, and already I am desperate for more. To read each story is to be involved in an exhilarating game, for which there are only winners.”

- **Brandi Wells, author of *This Boring Apocalypse***

"'I want to be,' Donald Barthelme said, 'on the leading edge of the junk phenomenon.' And Meredith Alling in *Sing the Song*, this postmodern Sears-Roebuckian catalogue of augmented and enriched hot messing scrambled transmogrifications, delivers fictions that are as sharp as the yipping yodeling angstroms of the molecule-thick edge hone of a samurai katana. These deadly deadpanned and panicked objective correlatives do indeed sing like the vibrations of celestial objects, like the nervous nominative notations quoted from beyond the quilted clouds. These are arias of the Seraphim hiccupping while high on isotopic helium."

- Michael Martone, author of *Michael Martone* and *Winesburg, Indiana*

sing the song

stories

MEREDITH ALLING

Future Tense Books

Sing the Song

Direct inquiries to info@futuretensebooks.com
www.futuretensebooks.com

First printing, November 2016
Paperback ISBN 978-1-892061-80-5

Cover art and design by Kat Catmur
Interior design by Tyler Meese

Printed in the United States of America

Other Babies

Some babies drink soda the second they are born. They glug it down. The sugar courses through their body. You can see the brown humming through their spider web skin. It shoots straight up to the brain, the hub. It clocks in at five past and gets to work. So that's certain babies. Other babies determine the cheese level of their surroundings within seconds of inhalation. Then their fingers form into little paws and they claw, claw at the air. This goes on and on to the point of burnout. Then some kind pillowy nurse brings a cheese cube and pops it into their mouth just to balance things out. Other babies are vibrating piglets. They have fleshy hooves. They have regular faces. It'll be a tough life for those babies, so decisions must be made. Go pig? Some babies go pig. Other babies don't. Other babies suck the life force from any adult human that looks into their clean glass baby eyes. The adult humans are powerless. They melt, get like a candle, dripping and lopsided. Their mouths stretch out against their bodies like wax. A lip starting at the shoulder and ending near the thigh. They try to lift an everyday object—a pencil. They can't. Their fingers are useless. They look at the baby and something strong happens inside of them. Other babies have the ability to chew gum. They find a way to move it around in their soft pink mouths. Gum on gum. Any baby who can chew gum is known in their circle as a riot. Other babies do not care to move. They lie like rocks from the moment of the birth. They lie like bricks. They stare up at the clouds and watch them slip across the sky. The clouds move like liquid, like milk. Other babies have four television screens positioned around their heads for total saturation. The outside world ceases to exist. These babies make friends with the pink cat. They think of stumps as seats. They aren't curious about anything. They don't ask any questions at all. Other babies are leaf dwellers. They prefer the dirt and they cocoon themselves in leaves. They bite a breathing hole through their leaf wrap. The darkness is welcome; no eye holes. Their bodies turn cold and tight, and then they bloom. Other babies hang on the rear windshield wipers until a member of a driving family says, "There's a baby back there, on the wipers." They pull over and pry the baby's fingers from the wipers; a surprisingly tight grip. Then they brush the flies and the grime from its body and decide to love it. Other babies can smell when meat is perfectly cooked. They let out a violent bark, like a seizure-sensing dog sensing a seizure. Ready the fork and the spoon. These babies end up kitchen companions, propped on the counter, maybe strapped to a cupboard with a bungee cord. Other babies look groovy in tiny jean jackets or tiny leather jackets and tiny leather pants. They wear groovy little sunglasses with an elastic strap. The plastic smashes their eyelashes. Their onesies are decorated with bones. Other babies pinch themselves and cause injury. Puffy arms and legs covered in sharp red pops. This condition is handled with heavy sedatives that cause a baby's eyes to roll back in their head and their mouth to go slack and they can't listen or learn or even eat, but they also can't pinch. Other babies are stubborn jackasses. They cross their arms and roll out their bottom lips and just refuse. Other babies carry small baskets everywhere. They exit the womb with a basket on their arm. Then it's time to fill up the basket. Gauze or whatever at the hospital, then moving forward anything else that is around. Packs of Chiclets, earrings, coins, diaper cream, eggs, crackers, tape. They carry the basket around and people peek inside the basket and say, "Oh what have you got there?" And the baby holds it up all proud. Other babies prefer cows over any other animal. They admire their tall bodies and large heads. They admire their twitching legs and the flies gathered around their eyes. They want to hug a cow's neck, pull the loose skin, have the cow not react. Or have the cow lick their chins very hard. Other babies read at a high level right away. They hold a newspaper out in front of them and shake it to flatten the pages. They lick their thumb and turn to World News. They get a serious look on their bald faces. They look out the window and think something then turn back to the text. Other babies do not make it very long as babies. It would have been better if they were born a bit older. They can't be handled. They make someone scream and want to crash the truck. Sometimes they are poisoned. Sometimes people have to live with having poisoned a baby. Other babies are very alive. They are in every room and every muscle and every eyeball. They are loud rushing blood. They are the arm or the leg of someone and that person can never shake that arm or leg, they just stare at it, wonder if it is really a part of them, or if it's not a part of them. They can't figure it out. Is that baby me? Am I that baby? It's all very confusing. They really want to grab and find out. They try to hold their own hand, their own leg. They feel their skin on their skin and they cry.

Steelhead

I pulled Steven aside at the party and said, "Actually this is the time to band together, not pull apart. This is the time when we should be trying hard to be good and remember to pick Gabe up from school and plan that trip to Vietnam."

I saw Gabe over by the ice sculpture and I mouthed *what*? and he squinted and Steven lifted my arm by the elbow which made me yank it away.

He said, "Get you into the car."

I said, "With all of your dreams, imagine this."

In the car I put all of the windows down. I looked in the rearview mirror and saw Gabe's hair flying. I saw a truck that looked like a pastrami sandwich. I said, "Can we stop for fries?" and Steven said, "You're just beyond," and Gabe laughed in his sleep.

It was fine to be drunk. I was glad about it. I said, "Goodnight Gabey" when Steven lowered Gabe into his airplane-shaped bed and then we went downstairs and I drank water and leaned against the island. Steven peeled and ate a banana.

He said, "That old babysitter was there, Caroline." I tried to remember Caroline. Oh yeah Caroline. Long legs Caroline. I said, "Why was she there?" and he said, "Her dad is on the board," and I said, "What were we saving?" and he said, "Steelhead."

Upstairs in bed I said, "Steven, it's time to save this marriage," and opened my arms for an embrace. Steven stayed where he was and took off his tie and I dropped my arms to the comforter and it poofed. I said, "Hey there but did you hear?"

Steven went into the bathroom and started brushing his teeth. I ran my tongue over my teeth. I could skip brushing. I could leave my makeup on. The other week I left my makeup on and I looked great upon rising! Steven closed the door and I heard him peeing which made me think well why bother. And then I heard him wash his hands and I thought well good.

When he came out of the bathroom he said, "Aren't you going in there?" and I just smiled and shook my head. He shut off the bathroom light and turned on the TV and said, "I just want to check something." I said, "What!" And he said, "Oh nevermind. I thought that Putin thing was on tonight," and I said, "Haha, what!" And he said, "Nevermind!" and turned off the TV.

Then he jumped on the bed! Like a wee boy! He jumped and landed on his knees and I said, "Hello!" and he said, "Uhhhh watcha doin'?" and I said, "Hanging around," and he touched my cheek and said, "You're looking nice." And then he kissed me and put his warm arms around me. And then he loved my whole wide body and I didn't think about his for one second.

Then I went to the bathroom to pee and I still left the makeup on because too much trouble! So much work! I use six potions at night. But I did rinse with mouthwash. I shouted, "I haven't used this mouthwash in a long time! It got crusted!" and he shouted, "What!" and I leaned out of the bathroom door and said, "That mouthwash is painful."

I left the bathroom light on and when I got into bed Steven said, "Are you going back in there?" and I said, "Ugh just leave it," and he said, "I'll get it" and got up and turned off the light. When he returned he pulled the covers up to his chin and shivered and I said, "Oh come on."

When we woke up I went to the bathroom and I looked pretty good! Not great but not bad! I called out, "Gabe!" and he appeared at the bathroom door with his hair sticking up and I said, "I'm loving that, the whole look," and he said, "What are you even talking about?" Steven came to the door and said, "I'm not making a dramatic breakfast, who wants cereal?" and Gabe and I both said, "No thanks," and Steven went downstairs loud as hell.

I spit in the sink and then hugged Gabe and I said, "Gabe, what's wrong? Why so limp?" And he said, "I hate parties" and I said, "Tell me about it" and he said,

"They make me feel terrible" and I said, "Right on there," and he said, "OK, just so you know," and I said, "Loud and clear" and then he pulled away and went downstairs and I looked in the mirror and said, "Today you be good."

Small Man

A small man walked out from behind my uncle's television once. He just walked out, my uncle says, and then walked down the hall. No big deal. I half believe this story because when I was a child I had a small plastic refrigerator, yellow and rounded at the edges. I used to put toy people or animals in there—maybe even a chicken nugget once, shh—and know that they came alive.

Sometimes when I tell the story about my uncle people think it's funny, but it's not. It's serious. Hello. My uncle was sitting right there in his brown corduroy recliner with a plate of potatoes. He was watching his favorite show about a family of tow truck drivers in Louisville and their drama and their highlighted hair and their dog Chipwich who had a seizure but is fine and wears a baseball cap with ear holes.

So the guy walks out from behind the television and my uncle just stares. Guy is a normal guy—not a gnome or troll or anything—just a little guy in normal clothes (though if you ask my uncle "what kind of clothes?" he just shakes his head like he's never described clothes before and doesn't know how).

The hall in my uncle's house is blue carpeted and the walls are paneled and covered in family photos. My cousin Byron's bedroom comes first on the left, followed by the bathroom (foamy toilet seat), and my uncle and aunt's bedroom beyond it. On the right side is my other cousin Luke's bedroom.

If you ask my uncle, he'll say he thinks the man went into the bathroom. But the hallway was dark—no one else was home—and it was hard to see. It was hard to focus, too. My uncle thought maybe he was having a stroke. He scratched his potato plate with his fork and then dropped the fork onto the carpet next to his suede slipper. Then he muted the TV.

He says he sat there for a few minutes because again, he thought maybe he was going through something. But after a while he got up and put the potatoes on the counter and turned on all the lights and walked down the hall and into the bathroom. And when he got there he checked everything—including the cabinet—and he didn't find anything, not a trace. He even checked the carpet for footprints.

So he went back to his television show and his potatoes and when my aunt got home from her bridge game my uncle told her about the man. My aunt put her hands on her hips and frowned and walked to the bathroom. She opened the window and when my uncle heard this he got up from his seat and went to see about it.

"Maybe he jumped," she said.

They both looked down onto the street at the empty sidewalks and their trashcans and the chain link fence with the bike lock stuck to it. My uncle took my aunt's hand and squeezed it tight. Squeezed it tight and then closed the window hard.

Scooter

I saw a man holding a gun to a dog's head and another man taking their picture so I stepped back and assessed like number one what is going on number two do I want to see it if this man blows this dog's head off number three what is the other possibility here. The other possibility that my brain came up with pretty fast I have to say is that this is a photo shoot for an instructional book on dog training. The title of the book is Do You Ever Just Want to Kill Your Dog or maybe it's Are You Holding Your Dog Hostage which could mean that you are not walking your dog or taking it out enough and that's the reason for the bad behavior. Or maybe it's You Won't Have to Hold a Gun to Your Dog's Head to Get Them To Do These 10 Tricks. That's the obvious situation so I lean over the fence and I say hey when does the book come out and the men both turn to me and the dog tries to lie down and the man with the gun nudges the dog back into a seated position. The man with the camera is crouching and he stands up and walks to the fence gets right up on it and looks into my eyes and his eyes are green and he says do you want to see something crazy? And I say well not if it's what I think you mean and I nod at the man with the gun and the camera guy looks at him and then looks back at me and laughs and says what no come on over, come on there is a gate here. I think well OK maybe I can save this dog we'll be bonded for life maybe I'll get shot in the process be a local hero get a sum of money. I go through the gate and I get in there with the three of them and the camera guy says come here, look at this. He takes me to the dog and he says Scooter get up Scooter get up. The dog gets up and its back legs are totally dead like paralyzed or something and the knees I guess you'd call them are calloused over. The camera guy says go ahead Scooter shake a tail feather, walk a while. The dog listens and starts going and is just dragging those worthless legs but is really moving, not slow at all. And then the camera guy says OK Scooter good job come back now and the dog listens. The camera guy says this dog doesn't deserve to die, but some people want it to die. Oh I see I say. So you are not killing it. The camera guy says no we are not killing it at all and the man with the gun aims it at the sky and pulls the trigger and nothing happens except for his loud whoop, his loud and joyful whoop.

Ancient Ham

Once a year the Ancient Ham crawls out of the sewer to sit on a curb and answer questions. People line up down the block. Before the Ancient Ham will answer, they have to poke it: they bring offerings—small sewing needles decorated with beads or feathers or floss. When the Ancient Ham reaches needle capacity, it rolls back into the sewer, sweating and shimmering.

Most questions are about health, wealth, or love. They must be yes or no questions. The Ancient Ham answers by bobbing left or right. Left is no, right is yes. When the Ancient Ham answers, people scream. They faint. They squeeze their eyes shut. They piss their pants. They dip their fingers into the ham juice that collects on the pavement, then suck their fingers and retch. Some people throw up. The air around the Ancient Ham swells with sweet breath. This makes the Ancient Ham teeter with delight. Get it real delighted, it will vibrate. Women clutch their hips, men flex their thighs.

This year, the line is extra long. The Ancient Ham answers then spins quickly to deter extra needles, extra questions. One question per person. The Ancient Ham predicts that a young woman will get a job promotion and she falls to the ground and grinds her butt into the juices. The next man in line kicks her lightly with his loafer. She gets up and hurries away, throwing up into her hands. The man asks the Ancient Ham if he should move to Australia like he has always dreamed. The Ancient Ham answers no. The man runs his hand down the front of his face, folding his nose onto his top lip. A small girl holding her mother's hand slides a twinkling needle into the cold, wet meat, then asks the Ancient Ham if it is stupid and hateful. The Ancient Ham answers yes and then no. The girl looks up at her mother, confused. "Stupid," the mother says, "but not hateful." The girl squats down on the ground and dips her pinky into the juices. "Just like me," the girl says. She rubs the juices onto her lips. "Just like you," the mother says. The girl looks up, lips glistening. "Aren't you beautiful," the mother says. The Ancient Ham bobs right, right, right.

Sample Sale

I was the first person in line at the sample sale. I could see all of the white and brown bags through the doorway of the warehouse. The woman behind me was chugging water and kept accidentally kicking my heels with her shoe. "Sorry," she said, and patted my back.

I looked over my shoulder and another woman further back in line waved at me. I shielded my eyes from the sun; I didn't recognize her. She turned and said something to a woman next to her then quickly tip-toed up to me.

"Hi," she said. "Sorry, what time did you get here?" Her face was puffy but tight, and the skin below her right eye was twitching.

"Uhm," I said.

"Nevermind," she said. She pulled her wallet out of her purse. "Here," she said, holding out $500. "If I give you this, will you grab a white bucket bag for me when you get in there?"

I looked down at the money. "Oh," I said. "OK."

I'd only decided to go the sale that morning.

Loren had forwarded an email at 12:46 am. "I'm not going," it said, "but aren't you looking for a bag?" I didn't know where she got that idea. Maybe she was hinting because all of my bags were old and stained.

I deleted the email then pulled it back up when I still couldn't sleep at 3:20 am. I thought someone was breaking into the house again. No one has ever tried to break in, but ever since I stopped taking my antidepressant I've been hyper-vigilant. I learned about hypervigilance in a depression chat room I joined one night after a few hours of looking out the curtains.

I folded the bills and pushed them into my back pocket. "Thank you so much!" The woman said. She walked back to her spot in line, shaking her fists near her shoulders in celebration.

I felt a hand at my elbow. Another woman was next to me with her wallet out.

"Hi," she said. "I just wondered if it wasn't too much trouble, if you could get me a clutch when you get in there? It's called the Molly clutch. It's tan and has a silver clasp like a V?" She held out a bunch of twenties.

"Sure," I said.

I took the money and slipped it into my other back pocket. "Can I have your phone number so I can call you after?" She said. I told her my number and she entered it into her phone. She walked away looking down and then I got a text that said, "Michelle, Molly clutch :)"

A small group of women behind me had started

speaking to each other in low voices.

"I don't think that's fair," one of them said.

"It's not, I've been to these, you can't do that," another said.

"Excuse me?" Another said. I turned around. "You can't be doing that, you know."

The group was staring at me and heads were leaning out behind them to look too.

"Yeah," one from the group said. "Why would you make the effort to be first in line then do favors for people who couldn't be bothered to get up early like you did?"

The sun was blasting my face. I'd forgotten my big hat. I felt sweat on my lip and held a hand over my eyes.

"I'm fine with it," I said.

A woman I couldn't see shouted, "Oh, she's fine with it!"

A woman fanning herself stepped forward. "How about this: I'll give you $1000 if you go and return that money and only worry about yourself."

The woman who had been kicking my heels whipped her head around to look at the woman with the fan. "You shouldn't have to do that," she said. "These women need to take responsibility for their own actions."

It felt like someone was about to spit. I looked down at my phone and typed out a reply to Michelle. "I can't do it," I said. "People are getting mad. Come get your money."

"She's ignoring us now," one of the women said.

"I'm not ignoring you," I said. "I'm telling one of them to come get her money."

The woman with the fan laughed. "Right. I'll believe it when I see it."

I looked beyond the group and saw Michelle making her way to the front of the line. She was holding up her hands. When she reached me she said, "What's going on?"

"That's one of them," a woman from the group said. "Lady, you're not respecting the rest of us who have been here since 4:30."

Michelle waved the comment away and looked at me.

"Disrespect!" A woman from the group shouted.

"It's up to you," Michelle said, touching my arm. "Do you want to get the bag for me or not? It's your decision."

"Not really," I said.

Michelle threw a thumb over her shoulder.

"Are you just saying that because of these bullies?"

A woman from the group stepped forward. "Now she's trying to force her! Is someone in charge here?"

A woman holding a clipboard at a check-in table got up and walked into the warehouse.

"Was that deliberate?" Another woman said. "Ma'am!"

When I opened my eyes the group was standing over me. A woman wearing a visor knelt down and handed me a small bottle of water. I drank all of it and then started to cry.

"I can't sleep," I said, looking up and around. "I'm scared someone is going to break into my house. I don't know why."

The women looked at each other.

"Has this happened before?" One of them said.

"No," I said.

"Do you live in a bad neighborhood?" Another said.

"No," I said.

"Do you have an alarm system?" Another said.

"No," I said. "And I don't think I need one."

The woman in the visor placed her hand on her cheek and shook her head.

"What time is it?" Michelle asked. "Hun, I'll take my money back now."

She made a grabby motion with her hand. I felt weak but I lifted my hip and slid her money out of my pocket and handed it to her. She stomped away. The woman who wanted the bucket bag was also there.

"I should take mine back, too," she said. I leaned onto the other hip and held up her bills. The group of women cheered.

"We're opening in two minutes!" Someone yelled from beyond the warehouse door. More cheering.

"You better move," said the woman fanning herself. She was gently kicking my waist with her loafer. "You don't look like you're gonna make it."

Zero

Even legs get wrinkles. This is something that never occurred to me. I've been lying in bed beside the dog on Saturday mornings looking at my arm skin, the skin inside of my elbows to be exact. I've been twisting it and smoothing it with my index finger, which makes it wrinkle. The man at the tattoo parlor said, "I can't tattoo a circle there for two reasons: 1) it's really hard to tattoo a circle and 2) your skin is so thin. Look at how thin. See the veins? See the little blue deaths? That's just going to get worse. See how you're constantly hurtling forward? I notice you want to sit down. Stand up and come with me."

I followed him to a back room. White buckets were stacked on the floor. A bare bulb hung from a brown string. He leaned over a computer and pointed to an enlarged Google image of a small, frail arm.

"Look at this arm," he said. "How old do you think this arm is?"

I took a guess. "65?"

He laughed and minimized the image.

"That arm is 12," he said. "Surprised?"

"Yeah," I said. "I actually don't believe you."

He raised his eyebrows.

"That's your prerogative," he said. "But I'm not going to give it a circle, and I'm not going to give you a circle."

We went back out to the main room and I saw a woman getting a large frog tattooed across her chest. It looked splattered. I sat down on a black leather sofa and moved my skin around. The man brought me a cup of Pepsi then went to help someone at the desk. I sipped and listened to the needles buzz. I tried to make the sound between my teeth—zizizizizizz zzzzz zizizizizzz—and dribbled Pepsi onto my chin.

The man finished his work at the desk and sat down next to me. Air escaped from the black leather cushion when he landed. He took my arm and began to rub it with his thumb, which was rough like a bad tongue. We watched my skin ripple and fold. He found a spot where it didn't, a section of upper arm above the elbow. He lingered there tugging on the taut fat.

"So," he said. "What are you going to do now?"

"I guess I'll try to get this circle somewhere else," I said.

I thought I felt him shudder, but he was just shifting to get his cell phone out of his pocket. He pulled his hands into his lap and sent a message, then put the phone back in his pocket and returned to my arm. He refocused his efforts on the thin places, the weak places.

"No matter what, it's not going to look good," he said. "Even if it looks OK now, it's going to look bad later."

"So what?" I said.

"You don't value quality."

"Teach me, pa."

He laughed and let my arm go. It dropped limp and careless into my lap and I saw all of its potential—the sweet meaning of zero.

America's Strongest Boy

The boys salute the red-faced man. They stand in a line and Bobby keeps his hand steady on his forehead. Five minutes later, the boys disband and Bobby returns to his bunk to stare at his lizards, Meat and Potatoes.

Bobby has to go to craft corner and is dreading it. The boys are working on a project that involves looking back. They have to compile memories and then express their feelings about those memories through a medium of their choosing. Bobby is giving some serious thought to clay. He has a vision of a clay tower with a bell at the top, and he can make something up about his childhood church, about the security he found in the sound of the bell, how it rang and rang. "I can still hear it ringing today, ma'am," he'll say.

Bobby thinks the prize for America's Strongest Boy should go to Potatoes. He's experienced extreme hardship (fell behind the heater) and has persevered (Bobby found him in time). But it will not go to Potatoes. It will go to that palm scratcher with the laser haircut. Bobby will clap but it won't be sincere. Then the boy will go around dousing people with Gatorade and Bobby will have to protect his eyes.

Bobby is emerging as a problem camper says the report tacked to his bedpost. Emerging but not yet arrived. He is saying pardon constantly to try to salvage the situation, but no one is amused by his refined social behavior if he also swims fucked up. He has to rely on a kickboard that thousands have spit on, so he's not totally committed.

When Bobby arrives at craft corner people are huddling around the materials table. A boy in a helmet is massaging a tin can. No one is even glancing at the block of clay, so Bobby reaches over and grabs the whole thing and then the counselor touches the back of his neck and says, "Ought to be thoughtful," so Bobby rips a chunk off and puts the rest back.

Everyone is leaning on their elbows thinking hard about the past. Some people are even sprawled out on the floor meditating. Bobby narrows his eyes to look like he's trying to understand something. The kid with big legs is lying down and looking up at the ceiling and he says, "I hate my own smell and I'm not even sure why." The counselor walks over and crouches beside him and says, "Use that." He sits up and pulls a pipe cleaner out of his pocket.

Bobby decides that his tower is no longer going to have a bell, but an observation post with a telescope and a man armed only with ego and rage. "That is my father,"

Bobby tells the counselor when she comes over to inspect his drawing. "He is watching over all of us, keeping us safe." She bends to get a closer look.

She makes an example of Bobby. She asks everyone to gather around. "What we're looking at here," she says, holding up the sketch, "is the figurative made literal. Do any of you know what that means?"

Someone is sniffling and then full-on sobbing. The counselor sets Bobby's drawing down in front of him and moves through the group to find the crying boy. He is very small, several years younger than Bobby. He is clutching an egg in his shaking hand. The counselor hugs him and he pushes the egg into the back of her head until it breaks.

At the end of craft corner, the boys line up their in-progress creations on several workbenches. The small boy sets the remnants of the broken egg—some yellow-stained shell mixed with hair—next to Bobby's tower drawing. Bobby clasps his hands and bows at the boy's work. The boy looks at Bobby sideways and scratches behind his ear.

"Thin ice," the counselor says.

"Who?" Bobby says.

"You," she says. She pulls her apron over her head.

"Why?"

"Please."

Everyone leaves together and marches single file back to central camp. The counselor takes up the rear and announces with a whistle as the group approaches each cabin. Boys break off slowly. When they reach Bobby's cabin, he stops at the sink first to wash off. Then he goes inside and lifts Meat and Potatoes out of their tank. They let him hold them, one in each hand. They stay perfectly still as he sways back and forth.

The following day Bobby returns to craft corner to find that his drawing has been vandalized. Someone took a blue marker and drew an arrow pointing to the man in the tower, and wrote next to the arrow: A PERFECT IDIOT.

The issue Bobby is faced with is that whoever penned the remark is correct. Bobby stands and stares at the paper and the kid with the big legs comes up behind him and swipes him upside the head. Bobby chooses not to react. Then the counselor is hovering over Bobby's shoulder.

"What happened here?" She says.

"Jealousy," Bobby says.

Bobby gathers up the clay that he saved in his cubby and sits down at the only table in the room that sits one. Then the genius with the broken egg comes over and tries to pull up a stool and Bobby has to tell him there's not any room and he'd have seen that if only he'd looked. His eyes get watery and Bobby remembers his sobs, so he suggests the boy work on the floor next to him.

After about an hour of Bobby ignoring the boy, the tower is really coming together. The base is wide and strong, the molded bricks are precise, the telescope is fine, and the man is nearly a man. Bobby decides to take a break and see what's happening on floor level. The boy has been staring at his pile of shells and hair the entire time that Bobby has been making artistic strides.

"What's the problem?" Bobby says.

"Nothing," the boy says, looking up. "That's the problem."

"What?"

"I think it's perfect," the boy says. "I think it's done."

Bobby gets low on the floor so he can take a better look. The yolk and egg white dried in such a way as to prop the shell fragments up on their sides; they appear to be balancing on fine points. The counselor's hair forms a thin nest within the fragile shell walls. It's a beautiful, hideous thing.

"Yeah," Bobby says, standing up. "This is done."

The boy smiles and claps in a small way.

"Now," Bobby says. "What are we going to do about my Dad?"

"What about him?"

Bobby motions for the boy to join him at his singles table. He pulls up the stool that Bobby previously rejected. Bobby holds up the small clay man he's sculpted.

"Should this look like my Dad, or like a better version of him?"

The boy touches his fingers to his lips. He turns his head and stares out the window at a tree for a few moments. The sunlight paints his face yellow.

"Like your Dad," he says, turning back to Bobby. "Keep it real."

The boy watches Bobby's hands as he carves out a thick mustache and a thick belt buckle. Bobby presses them onto the man and then positions him in the observation post so that he is peering out the telescope.

Bobby takes the tower to the windowsill so that it will dry out in the sun. He instructs the boy to place his sculpture beside it. They look nice together: Bobby's clunky tower and the boy's gentle shells. Maybe later, Bobby thinks, he can bring Meat and Potatoes over. Maybe this boy will hold a lizard with him.

"What's he looking at?" The boy says.

He's close up on Bobby's tower, staring at Bobby's Dad man. Bobby squats down and looks hard at the beady eyes he fashioned by stabbing his dad's head with a toothpick.

"He is looking at me," Bobby says.

"Wow," the boy says. "Scary."

The counselor comes to where Bobby and the boy are standing and squints into the sunlight at their work, then writes something down on her clipboard. Bobby thinks it is probably something good, but if it's not, that's her problem.

Spaghetti

Boil water. Remember when you thought it would be funny to take a tour at the Scientology Museum? They showed you a video of a pregnant woman carrying a large pot of boiling water and then spilling it on her egg-shaped belly. She screamed and dropped the pot on the floor and the image froze, then a voiceover came in: *A child can remember things from before birth. What can parents do to protect and benefit their child most?*

Don't fill the pot to the point that things can get out of control, but not too low either or else you'll have pasta stuck to the sides and a white residue that will remind you of your elbows at their worst—chalky and cracked. You never learned that you should put lotion on after the shower or before bed. When you found out that this was common practice, you felt like you'd missed something fundamental about being a woman, like you hadn't been adequately prepared, and that lotion was just the tip of the iceberg.

Add salt if you want but it isn't necessary. It might make you feel good though, like you're in control of something. You might notice your shoulders go back like they never have before as you sprinkle the salt with your fingers, making loose salt circles in the air.

Cover the pot with a lid to speed up the boil. Turn up the radio. There's an interview with a prison guard who became the star of a low-budget documentary series after taking it upon himself to prove the innocence of a man on death row, resulting in the loss of his job. "I never got married," the guard says. "And I never had kids. Sometimes I think of the guys like my kids. They can drive you crazy, but you want the best for them."

You'll hear the clatter of the lid once the boil is on. Grab a handful of spaghetti from the box and drop a few pieces on the floor, drop one on the hot burner, drop one between the chopping block and the stove. Get the rest into the pot if you can manage that. Use a slotted spoon to coax the spaghetti down, to move it under the water level. Some is going to stick to the sides; it's OK. Use the spoon.

Once all of the spaghetti is submerged, it's time to start paying attention to the time. Don't put the lid back on the pot. Stir occasionally for six to seven minutes. Listen to the prison guard describe shank types. Look at the squash next to the sink and imagine stabbing it with a straightened mattress spring. Look back at the pot and imagine pissing in front of someone else forever.

Once it's been six minutes, check the spaghetti. Use a fork and taste it. You have the power to decide how you want it to be. If too crunchy, boil for another two to three minutes. Listen to the prison guard say that he's looking for a job. "If anyone is hiring!" He says with a laugh. "Have you given any thought to another career? Maybe law?" The interviewer asks. "Oh no, not that, no," the prison guard says. "Advocacy?" The interviewer asks. "Sure, maybe."

Once you've reached your desired consistency, drain the water then return the pasta to the pot on the stove. Add a block of butter. Add salt and pepper. Open a jar of marinara and pour it in. The sound as you stir will be unpleasant. Lotion squished between fingers.

Taste the spaghetti. If it's bland, add more butter, salt, and pepper. Give it another stir. Once you're satisfied, get a bowl from the cupboard and use the slotted spoon to serve. Take your bowl and a fork to the kitchen table. Sit down. Hear the ding of the fork in the bowl. Take a bite. Hear your own chewing. Hear the prison guard say, "So much harm is foreseeable."

Lady Legs

I petted all of the hairy lady legs at the carnival. I put $7.50 in the meter and a slat slid out from the fence. I crouched down to get a good look. An attendant was on a stool behind me eating a pear. I didn't want him to be there. The sign said it all: no touching. But I had thought about it all day the day before and all night the night before and I woke up with thick sweat on my neck. So I petted them. They jerked and twisted away from my hands. I heard the attendant's stool squeak as he stood up. He came over and tapped my shoulder with a finger like a carrot.

"No, no, no," he said, wagging that carrot in my face when I turned my head.

"But I love them," I said pitifully.

He chuckled. I called him Chuckles.

He said "quit fooling around" and pulled my ear and I stood up.

When I got to my feet the slat slid back in place. I took out my wallet.

"If you do it again," Chuckles said, backing up to his stool and sitting down, "no touching."

The meter ate my money and the slat slid back out. My eyes landed on a pair of legs near the end, ruddy and dry and covered in thin black hairs. I dropped into a squat and froggied over there. The mushy knees clenched and released. I slapped my thighs so I wouldn't do wrong again. Chuckles was watching me.

"Do you have goats here?" I said to the legs.

"For sure," Chuckles said. "On the other side with the pigs. They all wear pajamas."

A thin peel of skin on a knee stole my heart. I felt my hand getting itchy and I slapped my thigh again. I looked up and down the row. So many colors and shapes. I love a right-above-the-knee area. I bit the inside of my cheek too hard and blood squirted out and I spit it on the ground.

"Now now," Chuckles said.

"I wanna bite them," I said.

Chuckles huffed out of his nose. "You'd better not."

It was so mild in the shade, my squat was comfortable, I wasn't tired. I felt good about staying forever, paying forever, until all of my money ran out.

"Is the rest hairy?" I asked.

"I never saw the rest," Chuckles said. "But I bet."

I tried to get a view up, to look up the legs, but the opening was too narrow. I wrapped my hands around my ankles and felt my own hairs, short and stiff, not silky.

"I am going to bust them out," I said.

"Don't tell me that," Chuckles said. "I'm the last

person to tell."

I pushed a finger into the dirt next to my foot. Easy to dig. I imagined all of the legs running free in a field, bodies above them, long hair flapping.

I found the thin peel of skin again. "How about you?" I said to it. "What do you like to do?" The knees clenched, released.

"I like to swim," Chuckles said. I made a little scream.

"They can't hear you," he said. "They're all wearing headphones, listening to the music or radio program of their choice."

I fell from my squat and landed cross-legged on the ground.

"How am I supposed to ask them if they want to go?" I said.

"Please stop telling me about this plan!" Chuckles said, standing up. "It's inappropriate!"

I curled my body into the dirt and pushed my wallet over to Chuckles.

"Can you keep feeding it?" I asked.

He bent over to pick up the wallet and made a pain sound.

"I'll feed it until my break," he said, straightening up, "which is pretty soon."

I closed my eyes and listened to the slat sliding in, the click of the meter, and then the slat sliding back out. I opened my eyes and there they were again, whiskered sugar. I rolled over and looked at Chuckles, back on his stool. His hands were folded on his stomach; he was asleep. His mouth dropped open, and a bubble bloomed and popped between his lips.

I dug my finger into the dirt, and then another finger, and then another, until I was pawing with both hands. The dirt was soft and stupid and moved away quickly. Before long I was reaching a hand under the fence and touching a hard heel. A leg kicked back and I looked up to see which one; it had freckled knees—beautiful. Soon all of the legs were moving, turning, bending. Eyes replaced knees behind the opening and I sat up to face them. I mimed removing headphones and the hands behind the opening obliged.

"Would you like to leave?" I said. I looked over my shoulder to confirm Chuckles. "It's safe," I said, turning back.

The eyes exchanged glances and the bodies backed away, paused in a mass, and then returned to the fence.

"We've discussed it," said a pair of hazel eyes, "and no."

A knot came fast to my throat, and my eyes burned with forming tears.

"Why?" I said, but I was speaking to a slat moving across shifting skin.

I filled in the hole I'd dug and smoothed the dirt with my palms. Chuckles was stirring as I stood. He licked his lips and patted his chest for my wallet.

"You missed it," I said, taking the wallet from his hand. "They want to stay."

Chuckles dropped his head to one shoulder and then the other, cracking his neck.

"I know," he said. "It's nice here. There's a pool. It's good here. It's better than a lot of other places."

I looked at his face, soft and round, and imagined it underwater like blue jelly, his body gliding behind him, his large feet flippered. Then I rolled up my pant legs and showed him my growth and waited for some love.

The Drug

Dana wanted to be cool with the teenagers, but they made her nervous. They hung out on the bench outside the park at the end of her street. When she passed their post, she sometimes said "Hey" or nodded. Sometimes they nodded back and sometimes they said "Hey lady." They were Polish, and she thought maybe that was all they could say.

She noticed that the boys wore wide, faded jeans and oversize sweatshirts—usually white or tan. The girls wore low-rise jeans with rhinestones along the pockets and slim hooded sweatshirts. They had earrings up and down their ears and jewels on their fingernails and frosty lipstick.

She started collecting those things in pieces. She started with the jeans. She couldn't find rhinestones, but settled for a soft, dark pair with pink-and-white stitching along the pockets. Then she found a big white sweatshirt at a thrift store. It made more sense than the kind the girls wore. More versatile. Then she called her friend Mel to ask about the earrings.

"I don't understand," Mel said. "You already have your ears pierced. Is this like last summer when you paid that guy to teach you how to stand on a skateboard? Or when you bought that lunchbox to use as a purse?"

"No, no way," Dana said. "It's a good look, trust me. I just don't know where to get it done."

Mel sighed. "The mall?"

"Come with me?"

"Hell no."

Dana took the bus to the mall after work and asked for three more on each ear. The teenager working at the stand raised her eyebrows. "Three right now?" She said.

"Yeah," Dana said. "Up the sides."

The teenager exhaled. She used the gun twice and a long needle four times and upsold Dana on an after-care kit and a variety pack of silver studs.

When she got off the bus she saw the teenagers at the bench and crossed the street to walk by them. Her ears felt hot and large.

"Hey," she said as she passed.

"Hey lady," one of the boys said. Dana stopped and turned to face them. "You got an outfit. I like the sweatshirt," he said.

"Oh, yeah," Dana said, looking down at her clothes. A girl with short brown hair with blonde high-lights stepped off the bench from her seat atop the backrest.

"Earrings look good," she said, cocking her head left and then right to examine Dana's ears and face. "You need really better makeup and hair."

"I know," Dana said, touching her split ends. "I'm not sure what to do with it."

The girl smiled and Dana saw that she had braces.

"I love those," Dana said. "Your braces."

The group on the bench laughed and pointed at the girl. A boy yelled something in Polish. The girl clicked her teeth and returned to the bench and punched the boy. Dana laughed. She didn't want to leave.

"You want something lady?" The boy said. He locked eyes with her and nodded once.

"Like what?" She said.

"Best stuff," the boy said.

Dana looked at him confused.

"Good stuff," he said. "Very nice. Pure."

"*Oh*," Dana said. She considered. She leaned her weight on one leg and shrugged. "Sure, yeah. OK." She reached into her purse and the boy stood up.

"Be chill," he said. "Come on."

Dana followed him into the park and behind a small concrete building. He looked left and then right and then over Dana's shoulder before pulling four small bags from his large pocket.

"These, all of them good," the boy said. "This least expensive to most."

Dana looked down at the bags in his hand, at the white contents that looked about to burst from their plastic shells. She felt her heart flutter and she lifted briefly up onto her toes.

"Medium expensive," she said.

"Medium for the lady," the boy said. "$70."

Dana pulled out her wallet and counted her cash.

"I don't have $70," she said. "How much is the least expensive?"

"$60," he said. "You have 60, I see it."

Dana handed him the money and he dropped the bag into her palm. She closed her hand around it and lowered it into her purse. The boy nodded at Dana and put his hands in his pockets and began walking back around the front of the building. Dana followed after him, but not too close.

When she reached the sidewalk he was taking his seat on the bench and she waved. The girl said "Bye-bye" in a low, funny voice and the rest of the group laughed.

When Dana got home she took the bag out of her purse and set it on the kitchen table. Then she sat down at the table and called Mel.

"What is wrong with you?" Mel said.

"Is it cocaine or heroin?" Dana said.

"How should I know? Are you crazy?"

"I've never done a drug in my life."

"Why start now?"

"Why not?" Dana said. "What else do I have

going on?"

Dana heard Mel pull out a chair and sit down. "What about Eric?"

"Dipshit," Dana said. "And a poser."

"A poser? What does that even mean?"

Dana positioned the phone between her ear and shoulder and untwisted the twist-tie on the bag. "I'm opening this drug up," she said.

"Damnit," Mel said. "Do I need to come over there?"

"If you want some," Dana said. She licked her pinky and dipped it into the white powder and wiped it on her tongue. "I tried it."

"And?"

"I don't know. Kind of sharp?"

"Sharp how?"

"Like a penny mixed with Ajax."

"That doesn't sound good."

"I feel OK."

"How much did you do?"

Dana held the bag up to the light. "I put a little on my tongue."

"That's plenty."

"Fine," Dana said. She re-twisted the twist-tie and placed the bag in the basket filled with unopened mail at the center of the table.

"Thank God," Mel said.

"Let's get our nails done tomorrow," Dana said.

"Maybe," Mel said. Dana heard her stand and push in her chair. "Let's talk tomorrow. I have to pick Jason up from soccer at 5. Don't touch anymore of that stuff tonight."

Dana hung up and removed the bag from the basket. She opened it again and tried to pour a little onto her finger, but made a mess on the table. She put her nose to the small amount that had made it to her finger and inhaled and felt a sting near the bridge of her nose. She pinched her fingers there and shook her head and tasted penny and Ajax at the back of her throat. She felt butterflies in her stomach and a rush of energy. She used the edge of her palm to move the mess into a small pile, then wiped the pile back into the bag.

She went to the bathroom and looked in the mirror. She washed her face and applied a sunflower reviving serum followed by a wrinkle reducing concentrate followed by a firming collagen gel followed by a thick night cream. She smoothed it over her cheeks and forehead and neck. She tugged at the skin next to her eyes to see what it would look like tighter and flattened the fat under her chin. Mel was always telling her that it was just a few simple pricks, or at worst, a couple weeks off your feet. She released the eye skin and the chin fat and smiled into the mirror, accentuating all of the lines and displaced fat. Then she went to the kitchen and got the bag from the table and returned to the bathroom.

She untwisted the twist-tie and looked down

into the white powder. Then she dumped it into the toilet, flushed, and went to bed, her heart beating like a child's.

Go Quiet

A stubborn hand is taking me away. I pluck a raspberry from a bush and launch it with my thumb. My ankles drag on the ground. The damp air wets my hair. "What in the fuck," I croak. Something sharp cuts my leg and it feels OK. I go heavy like a cow. I go heavy like a dead water buffalo, hot and swollen in the sand, stomach about to burst. The thing capturing me is breathing hard into my ear. It is working hard. If I had a soft bunny ear I would graze its chin and change its life. We would swim in the river together, my ears gliding behind me. I would dive under and pull it down with me and touch its throat gently with a rock.

I've had damaged ears for as long as I can remember. I usually cover them with a hat. Or I cover them with little discs that are like socks for ears. I smear them with eucalyptus oil and pat them dry. They require care. The damage is irreversible.

When I was small, my Gram liked to say, "What are you brandishing?" And I'd say, "What?" And she'd say, "What are you brandishing?" And I'd say, "My damage?"

We did this like a play. We performed this to each other in front of no one because there was no one else.

I see vinyl siding here and vinyl siding there and we are very clearly between. The mud and the leaves are familiar below. I filter through the darkness. A gray night cloud. A streetlight. A gutter. The thing cups its hands under my armpits and now that's the pull. I know my armpits are yellow. Maybe they'll stain, peel off like glue.

I dreamed of being taken like this. In my dream I escaped by opening a window and pushing my organs out one by one. I watched my liver run down a hill. We reconvened in a cave and my guts crawled back into my body. I thanked each one for its service. Then I slept in a ball and woke up in the morning and left the cave and found my skin tighter than it was before.

When I was young and first noticed my damaged ears, I pulled a plate from the cupboard and smashed it over my head then went out to the yard and walked around with plate fragments in my hair and blood dripping down my face. I marched from the yucca to the lemon tree and back again. I did this several hundred times, my Gram watching from the kitchen window. The rain plopped fatly on the patio. It seeped into the dirt and shined up the lemons. It soaked into my shirt and turned the blood pink and blurry. I pulled a piece of plate out of my hair and put it on the ground and stomped it. The rain dampened it and I used a rock to grind the plate bits into a rough paste. I rubbed the paste into the skin under my eyes. It cut, but just a little. I sat down on the ground and let the paste massage my issues. It burned, which meant it was working. I could bottle the paste and sell it. *Fine porcelain crystals exfoliate and tenderize.* I went down on my back and let the rain wash it away. It traveled down the sides of my face and some landed in my damaged ears. *Do not rub off; sprinkle water and let the paste dissolve. Can also be used to add luster to the ear canal.* The rain stopped abruptly. I stood up and dripped for a while. I wrung out my hair and some plate sliced my palms. I pulled a lemon off the lemon tree and bit it open and squeezed the liquid onto my hands. I smacked them together and the wounds tightened. *Lemon juice is a fine replacement for antiseptic. After applying, lick off to engage the antibacterial qualities of your saliva.* My Gram turned away when she saw that part.

I hear a sweet song like distant chirping. I am on the cold ground. There is a silk pillow under my head. Large shadows move around me and there is work being done. The thing is building or destroying or both. I feel places where teeth are missing. My fingernails throb. I think about how it would be not to be here. If I could be somewhere else I'd be under my gold blanket watching TV with the lights off. My face blue and my eyes soft.

The best place to be for my ears is under water. I dive deep in the ocean. I get in the bathtub and only my face rests above water. My hair swirls. My hips relax. Sweat collects on my lip and I lick it off. Water smacks against my ears and goes in and out.

And then my Gram comes into the bathroom and flips the light switch off and on. She says, "Are you going to stay in there all day? You're going to turn into a prune." Her words are muffled under the water and I smile. She flips the switch a few more times until I sit up and cover my chest. "The water is brown," she says. "You aren't washing hard enough. People think they don't need to wash their thighs, but they do." She drops a washcloth into the bath with me and I remove one hand from my chest to grab it. She crosses her arms and I rub the washcloth over my right thigh. "Good," she says. She turns off the light before leaving the bathroom and I wash the other thigh in the dark.

It is pure dark so we must be in a private place where I could do some harm. Total dark. Shadows more like energy blobs. I rub my cheek on the cold silk. I have a little thought: there is no wrong time to acknowledge power. Power as strength and capacity. Power as going heavy as a cow, the peaceful animal.

Are ears shells? My Gram stomps around the house. If she cared at all, she would stop with that. We slide past each other on our socks other times. We nod a greeting. She thinks I have no memory. Maybe a dog doesn't remember if you cut off its tail when it's a puppy, but maybe it does. The long part of the tail in some trash heap next to an empty potato can. Maybe it finds its way into the can and coils up in the starchy runoff.

I went to a therapist once and he hypnotized me. I was charmed into believing I was a baby and I shit on his chaise lounge. It came out my underwear and my red plaid dress. I don't remember doing it. I woke to him standing against the wall, his head next to the stone Buddha head on his bookshelf. His lips were white. My Gram hit me with a magazine when we got to the car and told me I'd never hold the cat again. When we got home, she took the cat out to the backyard and shot it with her gun. I went upstairs and filled the tub. "Don't drown," she said through the door. "Burgers for dinner."

I don't move, 6000 pounds. The night does not move. The sun has burnt out. Now I know it is building. It is a building, a house for me. I will escape out the window, organ by organ, lungs holding hands. Or I'll get old and bent in there.

Once in awhile I go fully deaf. Magic relief. I lie down and grind my heels into the carpet for a total pleasure effect. This is my prime. I imagine I'm wearing diamond earrings. I imagine I'm being launched into the air by a group of loving friends clutching a parachute. They launch me and launch me and I look down at their happy faces. They are all shiny hair and muted colors. They are people I've never seen before but they know me so well. They know I need this.

They respond appropriately to my signals. The fantasy ends when the sound turns back on. I stand up and walk to the mirror and look at my gray eyes, my gray neck.

My Gram does not know how to be. She wakes up at 3:30 am for eggs. She smokes and I clean up her ashtrays. She leans in a doorway and I dump them into the trashcan under the sink and then return them to their spots: the middle of the stove, the small table by the door, the windowsill, her bedside table, the top of the toilet. She coughs ugly. She is trying her best. She doesn't mean to point out my dirt. I assume that I came from somewhere but there is no evidence. I assume that she loves me but there is no evidence.

I smell a sharp flower. It pinches my nose, sits like a stone between my eyes, cools my forehead. I hope there are pebbles built into the walls of my house. I want to press my arms against them and see indents in my skin. I hope the thing knows how heavy I am, that my bed will need bolsters. If my bed is just regular I'll fall right through.

I try to lift my arms. They stay down. How is the moon nowhere? I scan up trying to find the sky. It's there because I can see weak dots of stars but the rest is a smear. Left, right, forward is a smear. Just the lurch of the blob now and again. It is incredibly busy. I admire that level of hard work. Physicality vibrates to let me know I'm not dead. I was a fuzzy calf once, brown-haired.

The eucalyptus oil makes my ears shine. Sometimes I hold a hand mirror in front of me and admire them. I turn my left cheek, and then my right cheek, and then I look straight on at the glossy peaks. I often think about cutting them off—just clipping them—the way I used to with the ears of my stuffed animals. I got badly in trouble for this. I just wanted their heads to be smooth. I kept the amputated ears in a plastic bag under the bed. I would take them out and arrange them on the floor. Bear ears and monkey ears and dog ears. I loved the speckled ears of the dalmatian. I would lie down and place them over my eyes.

The bag of ears was discovered and burned. I burned them as instructed, one by one. Which reminds me: I could cut my ears off and burn them. I could burn them anyway.

The thing is lifting my pillow and me. The pillow stays under my head. I'm in constant spinning. We're going inside of my building, my home. It is so much darker. I thought it was pure dark before but I was wrong. I feel my power. I do have power. I reach up and grab onto something hot and sticky and wet. I tug and tug until it comes loose. I hold it up to my nose and inhale deeply and it is a fish. I open my hand and it dances in my palm.

I do not realize that I am dropping until I am down. Is that flying? I hit something. I grip the fish in my hand and crawl on my elbows. Hard to move 6000 pounds but I do. I use my eyes for nothing but there is sound everywhere; loud, low notes I haven't heard before. I could have been swallowed and now I'm being expelled. I could be hearing throat. I sweat and I know I'm not dead. I am keeping this fish alive. I love it. I want it to be fine. I want it to have a successful life of eating and spawning. We're both breathing. We've got air around us. I think I can hear the river now. If I can get us there, we can swim—fish, cow, and rabbit. We can dive deep and go quiet.

The King

The cake is orange with vanilla inside. I think of an orangutan, which is not a chimpanzee. I look up at my mother and say, "Orangutan" and she coughs and says, "What?" I stare ahead at my father who is at the far end of the table. The two of us are the King and the Queen. This lady to my right is the butler. I look at her and shake my head but she's forgotten about her question and is leaning down to light the candles, right there in front of me. The candles are blue. The flames match the frosting. They sing the song. I watch a blue teardrop puddle on the orange cream.

When the song ends my mother puts her hands on her hips and says, "Make a wish." Where is the King? I try to find him around the centerpiece: a basket shaped like a goose. He is there and looking right at me but he is not there. I tip forward and blow.

I eat a gigantic slice. I get sticky. I hold my hands up and walk to the kitchen. I wash in the sink and look out into the backyard at the rose bushes. I whistle a little tune. It's all over. There are no presents this year on account of my performance, so I'm free to return to my room. I skip every second step. When I reach my room I close the door behind me and roll into a ball on the floor.

My warm nest, my nice nest. I like to swirl in the carpet. The overhead light is too bright, that is the only thing. The lamp is out a bulb. It's OK. I mess my hair into the soft nylon. I fold my toes over each other and fall asleep.

In the morning my mother is at the stove pan-frying sausages. She turns her head and smiles at me. The King is at the kitchen table and he nods at me. I nod a grand one back.

"I'm going outside," I say.

Outside I sit on the cement step. I grab the rusty railing and lean to grab a worm. I put it on the step next to me. "Your name is," I say, but when I look down it is gone.

My mother says "sausage" not too loud through the window above me. I stand up and go inside and sit at the island and eat four sausages on a plate.

The King stands up and stretches his arms over his head and takes big bird steps out of the room and I think about the clumsy osprey I saw on a nature show, clumsy but deliberate in the way it makes its nest. My mother can see me thinking. I switch it off. I take my plate to the sink and scrub it and wipe it down with the blue cloth then slap the cloth around the air like a nunchuck.

There is an event that we must attend today. It is the 25th anniversary party for my aunt and uncle. It is at a banquet hall. I get in the shower and wash myself twice and dry my legs until they are red. In my room my mother has laid out jeans and a t-shirt and a vest. I put it all on and comb my hair. Then, I put gel in my hair. Then, I get my sunglasses from the desk.

When we get to the banquet hall we dangle in the lobby while my mother talks to a cousin. I notice that the King is wearing his good belt with the Stockton Sizzler belt buckle. I check my vest for lint. There are photographs of veterans all over the place, lining the wood paneling. I point to one with an odd face and smile at the King. He doesn't see. Then my mother ushers us in.

The banquet hall is decorated with long white tables with white tablecloths and yellow daffodils. The tablecloths are shifty and shimmery like they're bad. We sit with people I don't know and my mother introduces us to her great aunt who might lose a leg. Then an old man with a soft face tells me that he read an article about how to make friends at the grocery store. I go and dance with Grandma. We really swing.

I bring a piece of cake back to the table. I look for the King and see him by the cheese looking at the floor. I watch him for a long time. He is not there.

My aunt and uncle give a speech and he gives her a watch and then they dance. They dance to "Brown Eyed Girl." Everyone gets up and dances, even the King. He's limp and looking cool. I hold the back of a white folding chair and sort of two-step. My mother's great aunt watches me with a little smile. She yells toward me over the music.

"I heard you had a birthday!" She leans forward. "How was your birthday?"

I keep stepping. "Good!" I shout back.

The party is a short one. We're forced out at 4 pm. The King is in the bathroom and I watch ladies in white button down shirts pull the white tablecloths off the tables. I watch one eat a cake crumb. My mother touches my elbow and I follow her out to the lobby.

A man in red suspenders is handing out white candles next to a large cardboard box. Everyone leaves with a white candle, even me. It is small and stumpy and tied with a yellow ribbon. I peel a little wax with my thumbnail and watch it fall to the floor.

When the King comes out of the bathroom I hold up the candle. He smiles and looks over my shoulder at the man with the suspenders. The man with the suspenders laughs at something. The smile drops off the King's face. He nods sideways toward the door and begins walking. I follow him outside, looking over my shoulder at my mother talking to a woman holding a small baby.

The King opens the back door for me and I crawl inside. He gets in the front and starts the engine and turns on the radio. We listen to the news. I look at the top of his head, the thick gray hairs, a few standing straight up, and I have to sit on my hands.

When Mom gets in the car she talks about the baby.

"Ruby," she says, twisting in her seat to look

at me. “Isn’t that a sweet name? Ruby? I just love that name,” she says.

“It’s pretty,” I say.

On the ride home “Brown Eyed Girl” comes on the radio and Mom loses it, she can’t believe it. She dances and shakes her fists in the air and is trying to get the King and I hyped up. I feel my armpits starting to sweat. I laugh and tap my foot. The King taps his thumbs on the wheel and bobs his head back and forth to the beat, impersonating someone clueless.

When we get home I go upstairs and change into my pajamas and go to the bathroom to brush my teeth. Through the small window next to the sink, I hear the familiar sound of the back door closing. I pull the small curtain aside and look down at the King seated atop the picnic table; he’s got his watch in his hand and he’s fiddling with it with his eyes fixed straight ahead. I watch him for as long as I can before I think he might look up and notice, but nothing changes. When I let the curtain fall, he’s still staring into the dark. When I look in the mirror, everything is the same.

Redhead Party

I was the only blonde at the redhead party. "Not even a wig?" Patrice said. I felt like a dipshit. I took my cup of vodka and cranberry into the bathroom. I opened a cabinet below the sink. A boxy makeup bag covered in sequins was open. I reached inside and took out a tube of concealer, a pink lipstick, an orange lipstick, a red lipstick, and an eyelash curler. I put everything back except for the orange lipstick. I applied it heavily. I blotted my lips on toilet paper. In middle school, my mom found some toilet paper I'd used to blot my lips in the trash and asked me if I'd been practicing kissing. She didn't know about blotting.

In the living room, everyone was playing a game with a large red basket. Someone screamed "pass the basket!" They passed it over my head. To look casual, I put my hands in my back pockets and found a barrette. I pinned a section of hair back. Something touched my neck and I turned to see a man with spiky red hair.

"How is it that you're here?" He said. I blinked quickly. "A girl like you oughta be," he said, "I don't know, on a banana seat bike?"

I wanted to punch his throat but instead I smiled as big as I could. He tried to kiss me. I pulled back. "No," I said, making the peace sign. He looked disgusted.

The basket made its way outside to the swimming pool. A girl with long red hair and bangs jumped in after it. Everyone pressed against the windows to watch her splash. She lifted the basket and dumped out many dozens of eggs. She cracked one on the lip of the pool and ate it. Medium-boiled. Someone opened the sliding glass door and everyone spilled outside and ran to the pool. They reached for eggs. I ran and reached too, and when I got an egg I cracked it against a tree. I held it in the palm of my hand. It felt like a cold little boob. I squeezed it until I crushed it and yolk stuck to my skin.

My lips looked perfect, I know it. Fox-colored and shining with the lick of my tongue.

Symbiosis

I was in a brightly lit fluorescent bathroom a few days ago and learned some things. Most importantly, I do have cellulite. A friend recently said, "Cellulite is a beast, and I'd like to make it my bitch." Not having dimples, I couldn't relate. Turns out I do.

Find the most important person in the room and make them your bitch. My body is talking about offshore banking, a Lexus SUV's mileage, the merits of linen. I sidle up to it.

"What if I told you," I say, "that I'm going to Morocco?"

My body holds its glass out for a cheers.

"Morocco is beautiful this time of year," it says. "Check out Nell's yoga retreat in Essaouira if you get a chance."

I reposition myself in the space. I want to scream that I'm a fucking DJ and get some respect around here. You should see me bring the house down. I don't take requests and my dance night is the best in the city. People line up down the block in big pants and don't plan on being home before the sun comes up.

I'm explaining to my body how we assign value when I notice in a mirror behind the bar that all of my features are too close together. If you have time to lean you have time to examine every inch of your being. An ad on my phone sells me on flexing in the proverbial sense.

One time I heard someone say they like commercials because they help them figure out what to buy. Hell yeah. That's what makes the world go around.

I've disembodied a couple of heads of hair and they live in the back of my skull just above my neck. One of the heads of hair belongs to a woman I saw working at a Japanese restaurant. The hair was fine and wavy and parted in the center. The other belongs to a girl I had a class with in college. She wore a navy blue knit cap and when she pulled it off, her hair would stand on end with static until she smoothed it down with her bony hands.

What I wonder is how I can take this all to a place where I find it hard to look in the mirror without narrowing my eyes.

I saw a commercial for a walk-in bathtub. That's not about beauty, it's about safety. But it's also about beauty, because everything is.

I tell my body that I'm redesigning my vestibule. Egyptian marble. My body looks very impressed. I explain that my inspiration is a tapestry I saw in Madrid that showed a giraffe crossing a wild river filled with golden fish and surrounded by small green birds. I want to recreate the sense of abundance and symbiosis. I am planning a classical waterfall, a circular shag rug affixed with Indian coins, and a ten foot birdcage filled with green parrots. My body offers to get me another drink. I say yes please, and hurry. My body returns with my drink and asks me about my vendors. I tell my body that those are strictly confidential, but the design is solely my own should my body be in need of a visionary.

It believes me and it wants me. We are going home together. We hold hands in the Lexus SUV. I look out the window at the moon, think about the blue it is painting me, the blue on my lobes from my bad hoop earrings. I use a fingernail to scrape it off blind. My body is telling me a story and I'm not listening. "Tapas," I hear my body say. "These little fried fishes in red sauce." I'm nodding in a way that communicates I'm on board with all of it. I'm impressed. Something sparkles in the rear-view mirror. It's my eye.

When we get into bed, we begin learning how to love each other and our subcutaneous shit. Squinting in the dark is enough to see some edges, some lines connecting us, soft and hot and in demand.

Whistle Baby

Clover is the name of the fat baby who whistles next door. She has a thick round head covered in black hair, and the small dent across her forehead renders her perpetually serious. She is serious even while whistling. The whistling started three weeks ago out in the yard. Clover was sitting on a brown blanket on the grass and her tall mother Shelby was crouched over the rhododendron. Very out of nowhere Clover puckered her gooey lips and a small wheezy whistle came out. I was in my own yard doing a thing or two and Shelby and I both lifted our eyes upon hearing the weird song. Shelby, who does not like me at all, then turned her head and gave me an amused look. I smiled and shrugged. Clover went on whistling and hasn't stopped much since.

The town people are clamoring to see her, and my relationship with Shelby and her tall husband Brett is worse than ever. It seems that smiling and shrugging at a whistling baby is the exact wrong response. This was outlined in a letter left under my gate Saturday morning. Here is that letter:

Sam,

We've tried to be good neighbors. Clover is a good baby, and a special baby we see now (and as suspected). A lot of people are interested and some TV shows too, but not you? Maybe we misunderstand. If you want to visit, please do.

S+B

A lot of differences between me and them. Me being a good neighbor is being quiet. Them being good neighbors is saying hello always and commenting too. Once I was out front doing things to the trees and Brett said, "You were wearing a sweater earlier and now you're not." That's true because it was cool out when I first started working but after some movement I warmed up. I said, "Oh, yes." And wow his face.

I want to be better and give more but it is not in my natural brain or my body. I can only do what I can do. I can try but if I fail I can only do that for that moment. But enough of those moments and you're stamped. Stamped as something wrong. Even if you want to try again.

I want to try again here. Here is a chance. Here is a whistling baby and I could do something nice like bring it a flower and say something nice. What is a good compliment for a baby that kind of whistles? Maybe *sounds like you're going to be a good whistler when you grow up*. But is the compliment for the baby really? *Sounds like she's going to be a good whistler when she grows up.*

Sunday morning I stay in bed for a while to get calm. I look out the window at the sun touching the yellow leaves. I can hear a thin whistle from next door; Clover is up. They are probably getting her dressed in something loud. Shelby puts that baby in loud little dresses and matching head accessories like bow sort of things even though that baby has just a thin layer of hair like a bird or an old person. If I had a baby I'd leave it in pajamas all day and put zero things on its head except for a hat the color of oatmeal if it was cold.

When I do get up it is cold like that. Socks immediately. I put the kettle on for tea and the radio on for some voices and prepare myself to go over there. It's my chance. I can bring one of the brown-orange lilies from the garden and hold it out to Clover when I get close enough. It's the kind of gesture people want and even demand and I can see that if I really think about it. I can see that doing what other people want and demand is sometimes the right thing to do.

So at 10 I cut the flower from the yard and carry it in my shaking hand down the path and out the gate and over the four sidewalk slabs and into their gate and up their path and to their door. I can hear a faint whistle and I'm ready with all of my nice stuff. I ring the doorbell.

Brett answers the door in blue flannel pants and a Team USA t-shirt. He smiles and raises his eyebrows extremely high. Without looking away from me he calls out "Shelbyyy?" And then Shelby comes in very nice sweatpants and a normal sweater. Her eyebrows go up too like someone tugged them.

"Sam," she says, a little strange I think. "Come in, please."

It is my first time inside and it is one of the best insides I've ever seen. The walls are icy blue and the floor is old wood and the table by the door is covered in seashells. I resist picking up a shiny speckled one and putting it in my pocket.

Brett goes to the kitchen for coffee and Shelby leads me into the den. Clover is in a bouncing contraption in the corner. She is going up and down and spitting out little whistles. We sit down on the beige sofa that wraps around the room.

"I brought this," I say, holding out the lily. "It's for Clover."

"That is so nice," Shelby says. "Perhaps I'll put it in some water?"

"Can I give it to the baby?" I say.

Shelby frowns and scratches her palm.

"Sure," she says, smiling finally. "Go ahead."

I stand up from the sofa and walk slowly to the bouncer. Brett comes into the room and places a tray down on the coffee table, then sits down on the sofa next to Shelby. Once in front of the baby I kneel and hold out the flower. The baby stops whistling and looks at me with big oval eyes.

"Clover," I say.

She tries to snatch the flower from my hand and I pull it back.

"Wait, Clover," I say. "Hold on."

"She doesn't really understand yet, about waiting," Shelby says behind me.

"It's OK," I say over my shoulder, then turn back to the baby. "Clover? This is a flower for you. I think your whistling is really something." The baby grabs for the flower again and I let her have it. She picks off a petal and puts it in her mouth.

"Oh, ha, OK there," Brett rushes over and takes the petal from her mouth then pries the rest of the flower from her chubby wet hand. "That's OK," he says to me.

I stand up and rub my face. Clover resumes whistling.

"I'm sorry," I say. "I didn't know she'd do that."

"No, no," Brett says, gently placing the flower on the coffee table. "It's no problem. That was very nice to bring that over."

"Sounds like she's going to be a good whistler when she grows up," I say. I sit down on the edge of the sofa. "I mean, she's a good whistler now. But at this rate, she'll probably be a *really* good whistler. When she's older, I mean."

Shelby looks down and then back up.

"My dad is a pretty good whistler," she says. She holds out a cup of coffee but I don't want it. She puts it back down. "We've wondered if it's something she could have inherited."

"*You've* wondered that," Brett says, then smiles at me. I smile back in a very correct way.

"Well it could be!" I say, slapping my knee. Too much. "Or rather, you never know."

"You never know," Shelby says. Her smile is thin and tight and she's shaking one leg.

"So," Brett says after a sip of coffee. "Shelby mentioned you weren't too impressed the first time you saw Clover whistling. Is that true?"

"I think I was pretty impressed," I look back and forth between them. "I think maybe I didn't show it, but I think I was impressed."

"You *think* you *were* impressed?" Brett leans forward. "Or you were impressed?"

Shelby presses her tongue onto her top lip and looks at me expectantly. Here is a chance.

"I *was* impressed," I say. I can feel the moisture on my palms. "I was very impressed."

"Why'd you shrug then?" Shelby says into her mug.

"I don't know why I shrugged."

"Shrugging hasn't been a common response," Brett says. "So we're just wondering."

"Is that why you brought the flower over?" Shelby says. "Because maybe you felt a little bad about shrugging?"

"Maybe yes," I say.

"Maybe yes," Brett repeats.

"We like you," Shelby says. "We don't know why you don't like us."

"I do like you," I say.

"We like all of our neighbors," Brett says. "And we like to get together with our neighbors. And we'd like to include you in that too, Sam. We'd like to if you'd like to be included. It's just that up until now it hasn't really seemed like it. Can you understand that?"

"Yes," I say. I look at Clover. She's still whistling, still bouncing. Her bright purple dress has a big yellow beetle appliqued near the hem. I focus on its cartoon face.

"It's nice to see you looking at Clover that way," Shelby says. "It would be nice if Clover could know her next door neighbor."

I shift my focus from the beetle to Clover's puckered lips. The sound coming out is just awful. It's wet, it's raspy, it's piercing at times. I want to get up and run but I don't. Instead I sit and I sit quite still.

"I want to be better," I say, looking back at Brett and Shelby. "I want to try at least."

"You're being better," Shelby says, her face softening. She holds out the cup of coffee again and nods. I accept it. "This is better, right now."

I drink the coffee even though I don't like the taste and I listen to Clover whistling even though I don't like the sound. I can see the crumpled flower on the coffee table and it makes my heart sting and my stomach twist and I feel hot and tired and confused and alone and I wonder if this is better, right now.

Mother Linda

What's true and documented is that when Little Erica tells Mother Linda that Mother Linda's opinion on the sweet hereafter isn't of value, is incidental, Mother Linda's face muscles tense and the hard spot in her chest grows harder. Little Erica says just put me in the ground, damnit, please just put me in the ground and Mother Linda says Erica why are you talking like that, why are you even talking like that? A question that's really a directive: do not talk like that. Little Erica is one of many who feel comfortable with the inevitably given their distance. Little Erica takes pictures of herself looking exhausted. These aren't intended for Mother Linda but of course she sees them. She thinks what is wrong with that child? She was a happy child. This is a way to occupy the sweet heretofore. Little Erica writes DREAD on her bedroom wall. She writes it carefully in black ink. She sinks below it into her sheets, mint-colored and damp. She writes GAL on her wrist in black ink. She pulls her hair into a ponytail and touches her face, feels her chin acne, smooths her eyebrows, peels dry skin from her nostril. Mother

Linda is careful with questions. Knock-knock, is it safe to enter? Mother Linda is fear, embodies it. Never will she die, and if she does due to some miscalculation, it will be a golden death. Chariots. Friendship. Family. Fun. Here on earth as it is. But life the luscious blanket keeps on giving. Little Erica, a gift. A little glass horse. Must be careful. How they move around each other. Little Erica deliberately slow, body slack, in counter to Mother Linda's tight and gathered herky-jerky. Not twitches, but almost. Reined in they are, but barely. Little Erica assuming masculine postures. Sitting legs apart, arms crossed, or leaning forward maybe, elbows on knees, hands clasped. Or thoughtful, thumb and forefinger supporting chin. Swaying, foot tapping. Grooving. A fluid body, one with space. Mother Linda the picture of uncertainty. Correcting her posture. Butt tucked. Hands clenched in lap. Shoulders too square; no give. Consequently, the air around them is sharp, confused. Chairs respond differently. Mother Linda sitting in Little Erica's red desk chair, trying to have a talk. Little Erica, frustrated. Stomach upset. The safest way to connect: medically. Mother Linda brings soda. Now there's maintenance, a reason for being. Mother Linda will check in with Little Erica in a while. It's better than not knowing what to say or how to say it. If you cannot separate yourself, take care of yourself. Make sure that you feel very safe and warm. Little Erica writes YEAH on her thigh in black ink. A positive moment realizing that she is off the hook. It's better anyway, to just stay inside. What is out there? Fear, suction. The dark room is a no hug zone. The wall says it somewhere. Somewhere lost now. Little Erica is cold, not by choice. Mother Linda, a drip of hot honey from a tilted spoon. Little Erica wears a jean skirt and a green bra. She slithers around the bed. Her oily ponytail slick. Mother Linda clinks around the kitchen. She turns on the television to have some company. Bond prices fell. She isn't sure about these pants, the new ones with the drawstring ankles. She isn't sure. Little Erica has said nothing. She is unwell. Perhaps she ate something horrible—fast food. Her poor stomach, her smallish body. What it must feel like. Mother Linda's hands on her hips, looking around. What was she doing? Ah yes. Little Erica checks her phones, sends messages to a few people. No, she is sick, cannot go. Seriously, don't feel good. She puts down the phone, gathers the sheet into her hands, tucks it beneath her chin. Everything dirty. Under her fingernails are many months. Mother Linda peels an orange and puts it on a plate. Perhaps Little Erica would like an orange. But, perhaps not. Mother Linda sits down on the couch and eats the orange. She watches television. She looks out the window at her flowers. Glorious. A perfect day, and, a terrible day to be in your bedroom under the sheets with the door closed. She shakes her head. A real shame. Little Erica cups her breasts in her hands. Not quite a handful, but close. She hears Mother Linda clear her throat. She writes ME on her arm. People would laugh if they saw. What people? No, they wouldn't laugh, they'd cry. Downstairs Mother Linda wonders if Little Erica just has to go to the bathroom. Should she suggest it? Maybe that'll solve everything. Our bodies give us messages that we shouldn't ignore. She washes the orange dish and puts it on the drying rack and then goes to the bottom of the stairs. She turns her ear toward the stairs. No sound from Little Erica's room. Maybe she is sleeping. But what if she has to go to the bathroom? Mother Linda begins to climb the stairs. The fourth step creaks like always. Little Erica sits up in bed. She stands and goes to the door and presses her ear to it. Maybe Mother Linda is just going to the bathroom. Mother Linda tiptoes on the carpet. She puts her ear to Little Erica's door. She hears nothing. She must be sleeping, poor girl. If she has to go to the bathroom, her body will tell her when she wakes. She will go to the bathroom and feel total relief. Mother Linda moves away from the door. Little Erica hears the movement and races back to bed. She squeezes her eyes shut and pretends to sleep. Across the hall, a door shuts softly.

Apologies

I rubbed the ear of corn until the kernels fell off. I wore a hot pink t-shirt dress with Daffy Duck on it. A man looked at my legs until I was sure they were gone. My hair was long and straight like a butcher block. This was in a backyard. There were pillars, white and nine feet tall. A woman with silver hair said that the outfits for the winter recital were green velvet. I remembered brushing a velveteen pillow with my knuckles while shopping for cups with mom.

A boy handed me a big chicken leg. I ate it and pushed my thighs together. It was a hot day. The hose was on, just dumping water into a soggy patch. These were days of water wealth. I was young with big teeth.

I felt that I had done something wrong, ruined something or hurt someone or killed someone. I felt a deep evil. I apologized with my lips to a picture of a nameless man every night. He was broad-shouldered with thick black hair. He wore a tight red shirt. I found him on the floor in the grocery store bathroom. He was looking up at me, so disappointed. I apologized on the spot with my underwear around my ankles. Then I picked the photo up and put it into my small bag. Then it lived under my lamp.

I knew I would have to apologize extra hard for the corn and the thighs. I imagined him peering over a cloud, watching me. I imagined opening up my mouth and letting him thrust his eyeballs into it.

Someone laughed and it startled me. I whipped my head around. The same man who took my legs away was holding a puppy in his arms, a fat yellow blob. He kissed it on the face and the puppy's ear flipped over. When the man winked at me I just watched that creamy ear, that miracle.

I went home once all of the chicken was gone. The house was quiet except for the TV that was getting louder as I walked up the stairs. In my bedroom I pulled the t-shirt dress over my head and got into bed. I inched the picture out from under the lamp. There he was: my very frustrated man. I smoothed my thumb over his shirt and put the paper to my mouth.

"I'm really sorry," I said, and tapped his face with my tongue. I fell asleep once my body was clean.

Insubordination

I am buttering bread when a man wearing a mask walks in and says "OK, on the floor." So I put down the butter knife and sit cross-legged. He says "Where are the others?" and I shake my head and he says "Who is all that bread for?" and I say "Me" and he says "Unlikely" and then Danny and Clark walk into the kitchen and the man says "OK guys, down on the floor." So the boys get down. I ask "What do you want?" and the man says "Money" and I say "We don't have any money, as you can see" and the boys look at me. He says "Where is the man of the house?" and I say "These are the men" and he looks at the boys and they both straighten up for a moment. I can see Clark's hands are shaking but Danny looks tough. He's got that firm lip he gets when he's fed up, when he wants Spaghetti-O's instead of a sandwich, the hockey shirt instead of the truck shirt. "OK" the man says. He comes to me and lifts me by the elbow. Danny says "Hey." I tell him it's OK. I tell him to stay down. The man takes me to the bedroom and says "Show me where it is." I say "There isn't anything to show." He says "Show me something then." I don't know what he means but I pull open the top drawer of the dresser with all of the jewelry. He peeks inside. "Something else," he says. I pick up the wooden box from the vanity and open it, hand him my father's gold watch. "This is nice," he says. He pockets it, then says "OK, what else?" I look around the room. I open the second drawer of the dresser and reach under the sweaters. I pull out a framed photo of me at Niagara Falls. "Have you been?" I ask. The man takes the photo and looks at it. "No" he says. "This is bullshit." I tell him I have twenty-two dollars in my purse. He makes me get it. Danny says "Mom?" from the other room and I say "Sit down Danny." The man is mad. He gets in my face. I say "Why did you come here?" He says "I saw the BMW" and I say "That's an old car. You can have it." He says "I know." I say "Why don't you leave?" and he says "No." I say "Why don't you stay then?" and he says "What the fuck." I am trying to remember any story about this kind of thing. About what people did and how they survived. "My brother is a cop," I say. The man laughs. "I used to be a cop," he says. He walks around the bedroom touching my things. He pulls the curtain aside and looks into the street. "Who is that?" he says. I go to the window and stand next to him. There is a woman parking her car. "I don't know," I say. "Yes you do," the man says. "I honestly don't." The man drops the curtain and sits down on the bed. He looks up at me and for the first time I see that those eyes in the holes are green. "You have green eyes," I say. "Don't talk to me like that," he says. I hear noise in the kitchen. "Boys, sit down!" I shout. The man laughs. I look at him. "This isn't funny," I say. He stands up. He stands over me. "I'm going to burn this house down," he says. I shrug. I lean on the dresser. "I'm going to burn the car." I tell him it's his car. He takes the Niagara Falls picture and throws it against the wall. Danny yells from the kitchen. "Sit down!" I shout. The man looks at me and I look at him. His eyes become narrow. "You are under arrest," he says. "For what?" I say. "Insubordination," he says. I shake my head. The man wipes his hand over the front of his mask. "You're a misfit," he says. He walks back to the kitchen and I follow close behind him. "Your mother is a lawbreaker," he says to the boys. "Your mother is a danger to society." Clark and Danny look at me. Clark cocks his head. The man takes a piece of buttered bread and eats it through his mask. I lean against the wall and nod. "She's a misfit," the man says, his mouth filled with bread. He walks slowly to the front door, still chewing. He pushes some magazines off the coffee table. I say "Goodnight, Officer" before closing the door behind him.

The Quarry

I went to the bathroom and stepped out of my underwear and into the shower. The baby waddled in from the kitchen. I looked out between the curtain and the tile and told her to go find something to wear to school and I'd make her an egg. When I got out of the shower she was in the kitchen in her dungarees and I got the water started.

I climbed to the top of the boulder in the bedroom and dried myself in front of the high mirror. I rubbed my feet into the stone and crossed my arms over my chest and held my breath for twenty seconds.

The egg rumbled in the pot and I jumped down from the boulder and went to the kitchen and fished it out with a spoon. The baby was on the floor harassing a centipede. I peeled the egg and handed it to her, and she put the whole thing in her mouth. It filled up her cheeks. She coughed and yolk and white sprayed out onto the kitchen floor.

I drove the baby to school and then headed to the quarry to watch the beautiful women dance among the rocks. Doctor told me I had to do this three times a week if I wanted to recover my balance. I parked on the lip of the open mouth and sat on the hood of my car and watched the women sway and twirl. I did not know where they came from but they were the most beautiful I had ever seen; tall and asymmetrical, with turned in feet and long knotted hair.

I was always the only person parked at the quarry to watch the women dance, which caused me to ask Doctor a good number of times if it was really the truth or if he was shitting on my house. He assured me that there is only one place that I exist and that is on firm ground.

The sun was bright and the wind very violent. The air smelled like sawdust and smoke. It whipped my hair around on my head and tapped the car with gravel. The dancing women seemed not to notice. I held my hair to the side of my neck and watched them trace wide circles in the air with their arms, go up on their toes, and bend their backs to touch the ground. They weaved around each other and then spun away and returned again.

Doctor said that the best treatment plan involved me taking one of the women home and making her part of my environment. The boulder was the first step. The woman would be number two. Number three would be to confine myself with both until I am steady.

I watched them move like one big octopus and couldn't imagine cutting off a tentacle. Then again, when you cut one off, another grows back to replace it. I stepped off the hood of the car and found my footing on the rocks and began to climb down into the pit.

I slid and stumbled on the gravel as I neared the bottom and looked to see if the women were watching me, but they were not. They were wrapped up in their motion, their eyes closed or to the ground, and it was not until I was at arm's length that something changed and one by one they stopped moving and looked toward me.

A woman with long red hair stepped forward and I thought that she must be the one. She held out her hand and I took it and turned to lead her away, but she did not move, and my arm yanked back still attached to her. As I was pulled into the group, the women began to smile in small, sympathetic ways, and then I understood.

Rita

I take a page from the life of my brother who crashed and burned going 120 along the East River on his green Kawasaki Ninja. I stand on the ledge of the building and sway. Nothing between me and the ground is untrue. Stacks of breath. I've always been afraid of steering into the guardrail, flying off the overpass, aware the whole time, changing my mind mid-way, thinking it's too late, it's too late as my last thought ever. I lift a foot so I'm only standing on one. The city sky is so bright. If I dropped a penny from here, would it kill? Would I see it slide into a soft head? Someone screeches behind me and I lose my balance and put the foot down. I turn and see Rita and she takes my hand. She has a pink rhinestone on her cheek—a diamond. She leads me back onto the roof of the building and gives me cinnamon gum. We sit down and lean against a wall below an air vent and she begins to ask me questions which are all the same question: why? I blow a hair out of my face. "I'm not scared," I boast. Rita shakes her head like Rita shakes her head. Rita is my sister and a good one. Rita Rita, I'd love to be ya. I used to stand on the twin bed and sing that into an imaginary microphone. She is so much younger but so much smarter, so much better of a person. Nymph-like, long brown hair, blueberry eyes, skinny fingers. I reach out and take them in my hand. "Do not take care of me," I say. "Don't take care of me, I take care of you." Rita's fingers bend. I cup my hand around her knuckles. "Don't be stupid," she says. But she doesn't know that I also drive fast. She doesn't know I drive barefoot, either, with all of the windows down and talk radio up so loud that it is like the voices are in my head, are my voice. I am in Mosul with the hot wind moving through broken windows. I look at Rita. Rita looks at me. Rita's head, so wide. Like the moon. I recall last Friday on the porch steps when she leaned over me with that head. She said, "wake up, please?" She whispered it. I said "I can hear you, but I can't move." She is small but she lifted me and dragged me up to bed. She was in her trench coat. I opened my eyes and saw it, army green. I said "beautiful," and touched it. Now it is getting cold and I pull Rita close to me. I lean into her and position her head on my shoulder and smell her hair. "I'll protect you," I say, "don't worry." She looks up and licks her thumb and wipes something from my cheek. "Thank you," I say, "there's wine in the bucket." She turns her head away from me and looks at the bucket sitting next to the door. "No wine," Rita says, putting her head back on my shoulder, "do you want to go down?" I shake my head and she feels it. I count the years since I've been here. Time is unbelievable. I've changed dramatically and

I keep doing so. When will it stop? I used to be scared of the dark, but not anymore. I used to think someone was coming to kill me. Now I am alone in the silence moving between black trees. I leave the doors unlocked and the windows wide open. I take baths in the dark, water sounds echoing off the tile walls and floor. Rita's head is the weight it gets when she is sleeping. I move it gently into my lap. Her rhinestone points to the sky. I hunch my back and bend over her, cover her as much as I can, blow my warm breath into her coat, and feel the cold air on my spine.

Treatment

The exam room is a mess and I feel right at home. I pull a magazine from the wall rack. A busty woman in camo straddles a cowskin bench. This is somebody's speed, I imagine. The variety of people in the world. I scratch my leg. The doctor comes in. He's tall and pointy all over. He sits down on the rolly stool and opens my chart.

"Let's see here," he says. He rolls toward me, reading. "You're complaining of… your leg?" He looks up and squints at me. "Is that right?"

I turn my leg so he can see the side of my calf. "I gave it a treatment," I say.

He gets his face close to the skin. "What treatment?" He says.

He rolls back and spins and opens a drawer.

"Tanning cream," I say.

He shuts the drawer and rolls back to me.

"Tanning cream," he says, grazing the area with a cotton swab. "Why are you using tanning cream?"

I close my eyes. "I wanted to look tan," I say.

He rolls away and spins again to the drawers. He

opens one and places the cotton swab in a small plastic bag and places that on the counter. He rolls back to me and pushes down my pant leg.

"You don't need that," he says.

He looks up into my eyes. I think about touching his face, cupping his cheek. He has a nice red cheek, shiny and tight. He motions for me to stand up. I do and he looks over the exposed parts of my body: my face, my neck, my arms. He takes my hands in his and looks at the tops and I look at the top of his head. Thick brown hair with a little twist and a little scalp. He probably jogs with a dog every night. He licks my left hand and then my right and I exhale at my predictive competence. He takes it as a sigh and licks the left one again. The right one he doesn't lick because it is up near my nose where I'm smelling what it means to be so sure.

When the nurse knocks, he flips my hand over and begins taking my pulse.

"Oh," the nurse says, walking through the door. "Thought you were done in here."

He holds up a finger and pretends to finish out the minute. "Just about," he says, looking over his shoulder. "But you can take that sample."

The nurse collects the bag and closes the door behind her.

"Sorry about that," the doctor says, slapping down my hands. We laugh.

At home I make an omelette and eat it and then

take everything off and stand in front of the full length mirror in the hall. I rotate my leg to look at the red, peeling skin then twist it back and look at the rest of me. I have a social responsibility to hate it all and I do. I put my clothes back on and in my pocket find the prescription with his phone number on it and the smiley face with two ovals for eyes. I sit on the windowsill and dial the number and put it on speaker phone.

"Hello?" He says.

I say nothing.

"Hello?" He says again.

I say nothing again.

"Hello?" He whispers.

His hot mouth froths the air or maybe it's my hot mouth that froths the air. I feel warm and swaddled knowing just what he wants. He starts to speak again as I'm opening the window but the wood squeaks and cuts him off. I feel the breeze and place the phone on my knee and watch the seconds count up. We stay like that for a long time and the sky turns a great purple. It's true that we're a happy couple, content in silence.

Tony

I smelled Tony's coffee when I got in the car and said, "I'm going to puke if I have to smell that all the way to Houston." He lifted the paper cup to his mouth and gulped a few times and I straight up gagged. Then he got out of the car and walked to the trashcan at the end of my driveway and lobbed the cup in.

"OK," he said, settling back into the driver's seat. "You're a nightmare."

Tony said it would take us 14 hours to get to Mom and Dad and Tony's kids. I was prepared for less time but it wasn't impossible. I rolled down all of the windows to get the coffee smell evaporating and Tony started scanning the stations. "What have you been listening to?" He said, his finger jabbing the seek button.

"Mostly rap," I said.

"What? No."

"You asked."

Tony frowned and jabbed. He stopped on the talk station and placed his hand back on the steering wheel. A cool looking yellow car passed us on the left and

Tony pointed and I nodded.

Mom and Dad moved to Houston in May. They are into the heat. They love to sweat. Mom constantly talks about how refreshing it is to sweat, and Dad is like her hype man about it, saying "yep!" They have Tony's kids now because Tony's wife decided to go study shoe design in Spain and Tony lost it. I flew the kids down to Houston and they were really terrible on the plane. The boy kept slapping me in the face with his sweatshirt.

While Tony drove, a woman on the talk station began explaining how to use pomegranate molasses and I really thought I was going to puke. She said to put it on avocados or zucchini. I leaned forward and pushed the seek button and Tony said, "you OK?" I nodded and kept doing some deep breaths and by the time I went through all of the stations and got back to the talk station, the woman was talking about kitchen thermometers and I realized that her voice was actually very nice, very smooth and rich. I leaned back in my seat and rolled up my window some.

"How are you doing anyway?" I said, turning my head to look at Tony.

"Oh man," he said. "Day by day."

He was shaking his head and looking straight out onto the road, but I saw his hands relax. I saw a photo of his wife on the internet a few weeks ago and she was sitting at an out- door cafe with a man with thick black hair and they were both holding up glasses of white wine and smiling. His wife was wearing a large, large hat, too large, white with blue stripes.

"You talking at all?" I said.

Tony shook his head. "No," he said. He looked at me and then back at the road. "What is there to say? I think she's mental, or on some kind of drug. She claimed I was the crazy one, which is funny."

"It is," I said. We passed an Arby's and I said, "Can we get Arby's?"

"Definitely not," Tony said. "We just got on the road. Did you not bring anything to eat?"

"No, I did," I said. "Arby's just sounds good."

We drove in silence for a long time. Tony hummed along to nothing. He'd started humming when his wife left, after I took the kids down to Houston, after he moved into my spare bedroom. He ended up staying for several months before finding an apartment of his own a town over. He hummed during dinner, while he did the dishes, while he read. He even hummed while he was trying to fall asleep; I could hear it through our shared wall. It was driving me crazy, but he was so fragile. He jumped at the slightest of sounds. He neglected his hygiene. He cried at the grocery store, an empty produce bag in one hand and a fat tomato in the other.

I asked my therapist at the time about the humming. She called it coping, which was obvious. I said I just wanted to know how to make it stop.

"Ask him," she'd said. "Ask him if he knows

he's humming."

So I asked him one night after dinner. He looked surprised, and then confused, and then scared. No, he didn't know, he said. "Oh God. Really? Am I doing that?" I downplayed it, said it wasn't such a big deal, turned on the TV, and waited for the low rumble from his throat.

In the car, I turned the radio up to cut the silence—the silence and the humming. It was the World News. Terrible what's happening. I wanted to fall asleep instead of listening but I didn't want to sleep while Tony drove. I blinked hard and sat up straighter in my seat.

"The kids are doing great," Tony said, seeing me stir.

"I was gonna ask," I said.

"Yeah, they are great. Cameron just started third grade, and Sandy is playing volleyball. Mom sent some pictures. They are really good looking kids."

I'd seen the pictures. Sandy looks just like Tony but with long, wavy blond hair. She's got the nose, the ears. I've got the ears too. She'll refuse to wear her hair up for a while but then she'll come to embrace the idea of elf ears and people might even be jealous.

Tony drove for six hours straight with only one stop to pee on the side of the road. He disappeared behind a large, dry bush and I squatted over an anthill. In Lubbock, we finally took a real break at a rest stop. Tony sat on top of a concrete picnic table and drank a coffee. I sat on the curb in front of the car and read some poems.

After a while Tony came and patted me on the head. "You ready?" He said.

I stood up. "Yep. Want me to drive?" He pulled his head back. "No offense," he said. "But no." We laughed. Tony's smile. I hadn't seen it in so long, I'd forgotten about his dead tooth. I was surprised he hadn't had it treated yet, and I tried not to look right at it.

The sky turned dark fast. We were on an empty desert road and Tony's face was like a rock. I felt like I couldn't look at the road, right at it. It was making me confused. I looked down at my lap and then at the glove-box and then at Tony's hands.

"You feel OK when you wake up in the morning?" I said.

Tony looked at me and frowned.

"What do you mean?" He said.

"Do you feel like you want to get out of bed?"

"Not really," Tony said. "Does anyone?"

"Yeah," I said. "I think so."

"Hm," Tony said. "I can't remember ever feeling that way. Even before. I'm not crazy about waking up. I never feel well-rested. Never have."

"I'm feeling better these days," I said. "When I wake up, I feel more prepared."

Tony nodded and looked at me.

"You didn't for a while?"

"For a long time," I said.

"Yeah," Tony said. "I get that."

The radio was getting fuzzy. I couldn't hear much. I could hear some horns. Tony turned down the volume but not all the way. I could remember very little about growing up, but a clear memory is Tony squirting mustard on the new carpet and everyone going insane. Even the carpet guy who had just installed it and the neighbor who was over looking at the hydrangeas went insane. Tony was so quiet while everyone freaked out, but there were tears rolling down his face, down his fat cheeks. He looked at me and I made a stupid face and he kept crying but he was laughing too. And then in bed later I cried so hard that the next morning my eyes were swollen shut. When I went downstairs, everyone looked at me and I said I got cat hairs in them. But really I'd been trying to cry for Tony, take Tony's cry.

It was almost midnight when we arrived in Houston. I sat up in my seat and looked out the window, looked up through the windshield at the buildings. "Damn," I said. "You think Mom and Dad like big city living?" Tony laughed and my heart thumped 1-2-3. My heart murmur. I touched my sternum and held in a breath.

"They don't live right in here," Tony said. "I thought it would be cool to drive through though."

When we reached the suburbs, we drove slowly through the silent streets. I pointed out a cute lamp post and then noticed that there was one in front of every house. Tony looked down at the GPS on his phone. "It should be up here on the right," he said, squinting at numbers on mailboxes and curbs. "That's it," he said. "There."

It was a big brick thing. Brick all over, plus brick borders around the doors and the windows and the garage. It had a fortress vibe, but there were blue hydrangeas to lighten the mood. We parked out front next to the driveway and Tony turned off his lights.

"I guess I didn't have a plan," Tony said. "It's too late to wake them up."

The house was dark except for a small bulb over the front door and the lamp post. We stared at the house, watched it like a TV. Tony was looking past me, over my shoulder.

"They are in there right now, sleeping," Tony said. "So strange."

I kept my eyes on the house because I didn't want to turn and see Tony's face. His eyes would be tired and watery. I guessed which window was Mom and Dad's, which window was Cameron's and which was Sandy's. I guessed where the kitchen was and the den. I visualized Sandy's kneepads on the stairs and Cameron's backpack toppled on the floor. Beige carpeting. Blue patterned wallpaper. I spoke into the glass.

"Do you want to go somewhere else?" I said. "Or stay here?"

"Stay here," Tony said. "Is that OK?"

"Yeah, that's fine," I said. I looked down at the floormat and picked up my jean jacket and pulled it up over my shoulders. "I'm going to get some sleep though."

"Sure thing," Tony said.

I just wanted to close my eyes and go to sleep and not look at Tony, but something pulled at my neck from deep in my skull and forced me. I felt my head turning, my spine twisting, my hair sticking and shifting on the leather headrest. My eyes widened and landed on Tony's face. His eyes were soft and dry, and his dead tooth was like a gray pearl.

Celebrate

The sun through the trees patterns me like a leopard and I creep. The jungle floor is covered in cell phones. I pick one up and say, "Hello?" A small voice says, "My temples are the color of an old plum." I drop the phone and look at my knees, which are the color of pea soup. I move wobbly in the direction of the sound of water. I let my legs be strange. Michael Douglas is my safe actor. When I see him or even think of him I feel safe and secure. I think of Michael Douglas. I think of him in a gray suit with his gray hair slicked back. He is sitting at a long dining room table with a soufflé dish of duck liver mousse in front of him. "Cheers to the champions," he says, raising a glass of red wine. "This is our year, boys." My legs are covered in red splotches, itchy bites. They are covered in hair. It's satisfying to adjust. My cat Shrimpy is at home, alone. She is orange and I find a leaf that resembles her head and stick it to my cheek. Sweat shines the creases of my body and pools at my feet. A water baby. I had a water baby. You fill the rubber doll with warm water so it feels soft and you want to nurture it. When it gets cold forget about it. Michael Douglas smiles. "Celebrate," he says. The sound of the water is around the tree. I pick up speed and on a leap grab a cell phone from the ground and chuck it. Behind the tree there is no water but more trees. I laugh and drool. A rabbit in the distance. It jumps through a shiny silver hoop. It jumps again and I see that its feet are all bloody. I reach out for it but I can't reach. Because it's in the distance. A sharp silver arrow flies under it. I crouch down on the ground just to think for a second, to rub my fingers over the keypads. Some are a little greasy. That is great news as far as softness is concerned. I make the sign of the cross and hail the rabbit. Supreme soft baby from the planet of Silk. I lie down on top of the cell phones and something wet drops into my right eye. I blink as slow as I can. I get as low as I can. I celebrate.

Hombres

The man with the children's sneakers keeps losing turkey from his sandwich, so I give him an up-nod like *hey man.* He stops with his mouth full of turkey and looks at me and nods multiple times fast like *yeah yeah yeah* and points to the bathroom and takes a step forward and his children's sneaker ends up kind of sideways. He grips his knee and drops his sandwich. A woman turns from the bar and the man holds up a hand so the woman turns back to her friend and shrugs. The man looks up at me and mouths something and I push my tongue into my top lip trying to understand. He mouths it again and then reaches down for the sandwich, one hand on the sideways knee. He gets the sandwich and turkey is going everywhere, all over the floor, and he slaps it on a tall round table and turkey goes all over that too; it's a serious mess. He's red in the face and creaked up and he looks at me again and does the mouth and I see what he's saying, he's saying, *What's the deal what's the deal what's the deal?* I start shaking my head, I frown without trying, because nothing's the deal. He stands up straight and shakes out the leg and his mouth is slack and the turkey is a real situation. He lifts the baseball cap off his head and rubs his hand on his hair, rubs it in circles, then puts the hat back on and adjusts the hat and some sweaty hair sticks out the front. *What's the deal?* He mouths. *What's the deal?* He starts moving toward me, starts limping sort of, and I guess I could stand seeing his red face up close so I let him keep coming. He's got his eyes on me and I've got my eyes on him and on the sandwich and someone has just noticed it, someone thinking maybe they'll take the table, they are calling over a waitress to see about it but after more thought, nevermind. He is getting close, he is a big red thumb, he is looking me in the eye then as he passes he looks away and says into my shoulder, "Come on, come on." I turn and he pushes into the Hombres door. I wait a few moments then go to the Hombres door and push it with my fingertips just a crack and I hear the squeak of the children's sneakers. "Hey," he says. "That you?" I see a sweaty handprint on the mirror and step inside. "It's me," I say and slide off my shoes. "Take off those shoes," I say, "and let's dance."

Hot House

Jody gave Scott her virginity in the backseat of Scott's RAV4. Her blood stained Scott's basketball jersey, and he showed his friends before hiding the jersey in the attic. He invited Jody over to his Grandma Chet's house the next week to watch TV. They sat on the brown velour sofa and Jody pushed her feet into the thick carpet and felt the beige fibers mush between her toes. Scott drank a Spicy Hot V8.

"Sup girl?" he said, a tomato mustache accentuating his blonde stubble.

Jody shrugged and rubbed her chin on her shoulder. Scott ran his pinky up and down her thigh, then licked the tip of his finger and pushed it into her leg while making a sizzling sound. He smiled and his braces glinted. Jody pulled her legs up onto the sofa, leaned into Scott, and closed her eyes.

When she woke, Scott was not there and she was sweating. She pressed her dry lips together and let them peel apart slowly. She wondered where Scott was and if she was his girlfriend. Then he returned with a bowl of soup. He held it out to her and told her she needed it for her strength. She laughed and wiped her hands on her blue t-shirt, then took the bowl with two hands. She drank from it and chewed the tiny chicken cubes slowly while Scott sat and watched, his hands folded in the lap of his basketball shorts.

A big van pulled up to the curb outside and Scott leaned to look through a slit in the curtains.

"That's Chet," he said. "I'll be back, don't go nowhere."

He walked out of the living room and opened the front door and went outside. Jody stood and peeked through the curtains. A young man stepped out of the driver's side door and went around to the other side of the van. He opened the sliding door and a large, soft woman appeared. The man took one of Grandma Chet's hands and Scott took the other. They grabbed her elbows too. She made her way down a small ramp that folded out from the bottom of the van, and the young man waved good-bye. Scott began leading his Grandma up the concrete path and Jody ran to hold open the screen door.

Grandma Chet looked up and frowned, then looked at Scott and shook her head.

"That's Jody," Scott said.

Jody smiled and waved but Grandma Chet ignored her. When Scott and Grandma Chet reached the front steps, she tried again.

"Hi, I'm Jody," she said, extending her hand.

Grandma Chet said "excuse me" and hobbled past her.

Scott took Grandma Chet to her room and got her into bed while Jody leaned against the wall in the hallway and bit her thumbnail. Through the crack in the bedroom door, she watched Scott smooth a blanket over his Grandma's body. Once she was comfortable, she pointed and Scott opened her purse and removed some bills, then tucked them under the elastic of his shorts.

When he closed the bedroom door behind him, he saw Jody and made the quiet sign then went to her and humped her leg. She used her elbow to shove him off.

"Your Grandma doesn't like me," she whispered.

"She's a boss," Scott whispered back. "She don't like nobody."

He led the way back to the TV room and flipped through the channels before settling on *The Ricki Lake Show*. The episode was about teenage girls who got breast implants in Mexico without their parents' consent. An image of one girl's breasts with the nipples blurred out appeared on the screen. The breasts were lopsided and covered in tiny red dots. The left breast had a bulge at the bottom where the implant bag was protruding. Jody winced. Scott licked his pinky and poked Jody's right breast while making the sizzling sound. Jody slapped his hand away.

"Stop," she said.

Scott whimpered. He pawed at Jody's chest. She

stood up and crossed her arms.

"Do you even like me?" She said.

"Keep your voice down," Scott said. "And come here."

Jody rolled her eyes and walked to the kitchen. She took a glass from the dish rack and filled it with water and drank it all down in one gulp. Then she filled the glass again and drank that too.

Scott came up behind her and placed his hands on her hips, and she spun around and coughed. Water came out of her throat and wet Scott's face. He squinted and wiped it away.

"Yo that's disgusting," he said.

"Your fault," Jody said. "And you didn't answer my question."

"What question?"

"Do you like me?"

Scott lifted the bottom of his t-shirt and used it to wipe sweat from his forehead. Jody's eyes went to the thin brown hairs below his yellow-white belly button.

"Last week was cool," he said. "But now you act like you're too good."

Jody's mouth dropped open. She closed it and collected saliva on her tongue and spit on Scott's shirt. He looked down at the wet spot and pushed his eyebrows together, then grabbed a wooden spoon from the utensil jar next to the sink. He lunged at Jody and slapped her arm with the spoon. She screamed and looked down at the blooming red mark. Grandma Chet began to yell through her bedroom door.

"What the hell's going on out there?!"

"Nothin' Grandma!" Scott shouted. He turned to Jody and raised the spoon again. She jumped into the hallway, then pushed through the screen door and ran into the street.

Scott burst outside after her and stood on the front steps breathing hard and flashing his braces. Grandma Chet followed close behind, stumbling through the doorway and grabbing his shoulder. She leaned her weight on him and said something into his ear and he laughed and nodded. Jody watched him take her back inside the hot house. Before he closed the door, Grandma Chet reached a thick hand behind her back and flipped Jody off. Scott turned his head just in time to see Jody flip the bird back. He raised two middle fingers in response—one aimed at Jody and one at his Grandma—and there was something like peace in the air.

Hellsure

Catherine on a wormless morning, praying to God. She found some hellsure sinners on her man's computer. There was a pink pair of hooved women in a bathtub, and then a woman and double-dose of man bent on a grand stairway, their surroundings aglow in flamingo wallpaper. She dragged them to the trash bin on the desktop while gripping her thigh.

The house smelled like woodsmoke. She stood and felt dizzy. She walked quickly to the bathroom and leaned against the sink and lifted a piece of dusty sea glass from the dish below the mirror. She gripped it in her palm and felt that it was about to cut her, which would be an appropriate penance. But it refused and she felt like scum. She gave herself a vicious look and moved on to the kitchen, to the egg her man had boiled and left. She regarded it on the butcher block and felt the desire to lob it, watch it rise and fall by her own hand. But instead she dropped it gently into the sink, watched it disappear with a *thh* into the disposal.

She wasn't hungry, anyway. She let the sun fall

over her face and she closed her eyes. She prayed again. "Heavenly Father," she started aloud, her hands clasped at her chest. "Help me understand." She opened her eyes expecting something, maybe a divine animal with a message. But it was just the window above the sink, same as ever, dirt on the sill.

At one time he had been a small boy. She thought of the only picture she'd seen from his childhood. He wore a little brimmed hat and pulled a toy wagon. And now he searched for hybrids: "pigwoman," "goatwoman," "manwoman," "beastwoman." The two in the bathtub had soft snouts in addition to the hooves. Imagining his organized socks and penny box, Catherine almost laughed. But it was as if there was a mirror and she could see herself in it, looking ugly and confused, and so she stopped and gathered herself up. Without thinking she grabbed a rag and pushed it against the counter.

What if she could vanish her head into the waves and get away from the responsibility? The thought scared her. It would be cold and black and loud. Well, temporarily. She breathed in and out and her heart rate slowed, the room came back into focus, and the towel in her hand felt strange. Stepping away from it and the counter, she felt a surge of energy and walked to the library, pulled out the desk chair, and sat again in front of the computer.

She opened the browser and placed the cursor in the search box. She typed what came first to mind—"man-man"—and hit return. The results were cowboys with proud smiles. She clicked through image after image: broad bodies atop horses, tan fathers lassoing nothing, bearded pairs in chaps and bolo ties. She reached a hand forward and pushed the button to turn off the monitor, shook her head as if removing a leaf from her hair, and stood up.

In the bathtub, she watched her leg hairs dance below the surface of the water. She lifted the razor from the lip of the tub and made long, soapless strokes. With a hairless body, she would glide easily into the waves for her head's rest. Rather than the scene frightening her as it had before, she experienced a wash of yellow joy. She felt sweet and smooth all over.

"Catherine?" Her man called from the hall.

"In here," she shouted, her words bouncing off the walls.

He knocked gently on the door.

"Is there dinner?" He said to the wood.

Her toes slipped and splashed.

"Why don't you come in?" She said.

A pause, and then the slow turn of the knob, and then the brown door sideways. Her man approached the tub, his eyes on hers, then dropped the toilet lid and sat down.

Catherine looked at him, examined him from head to toe. He appeared tired, impatient. He rubbed a dry spot on his hand with his thumb. His work turned him dusty. His boots were swollen, cracked, his loaf of foot about to burst through the stretched laces. Catherine tried to imagine the taste of his lips. It had been too long to know for sure, but probably beer and clay.

"What's it all about?" He said. He kept his eyes on Catherine's. They didn't drop or shiver.

Catherine smiled. She fluttered her lashes, let them rest briefly on her lower lids, bit her fat bottom lip. "Oink," she said, and laughed.

Her man scrunched up his face. "Pardon me?" He said. He pressed a hand into his knee like he was ready to push himself up.

Catherine twisted her body and squished her large breasts against the porcelain.

"Oink," she said, again. "*Oink oink.*"

Her man stood up, his mouth like he'd tasted trash.

"I don't know what this is," he said, pointing. "But I will not tolerate it. When you're ready, you get out of that tub and explain yourself."

He left the bathroom, the brown door slapping shut behind him.

Catherine laughed again and rose a wet hand to her mouth. Then she lifted her fingers to her nose, pinched it closed, and dropped her head below the water. She opened her mouth. Water and hair rushed into her throat and she sat up quickly, coughing and spitting. Once she caught her breath, she drained the tub and dried herself, blew out the candles, and walked calmly down the dark hallway, ready to explain who she was.

Versions of the these stories have appeared in the following publications:

Other Babies - *The Fanzine*
Small Man - *Storm Cellar*
Scooter - *SmokeLong Quarterly*
Ancient Ham - *Tin House*
Redhead Party - *People Holding*
Whistle Baby - *Cooper Street*
Insubordination - *Spork*

Special thanks to Kevin Sampsell, Bianca Flores, Kat Catmur, Wendy C. Ortiz, Loren Gomez, Ben Loory, Myriam Gurba, J. Ryan Stradal, Bud Smith, Kathy Fish, Brandi Wells, Michael Martone, Noy Holland, Amelia Gray, Joy Partridge, Mom, Dad, Jonathan Hudson, Marina Santos, the Allings, the Krauses, and all of my sweet friends. Can never thank you enough Roderick McClain. Oliver Alling – oh the towering feeling.

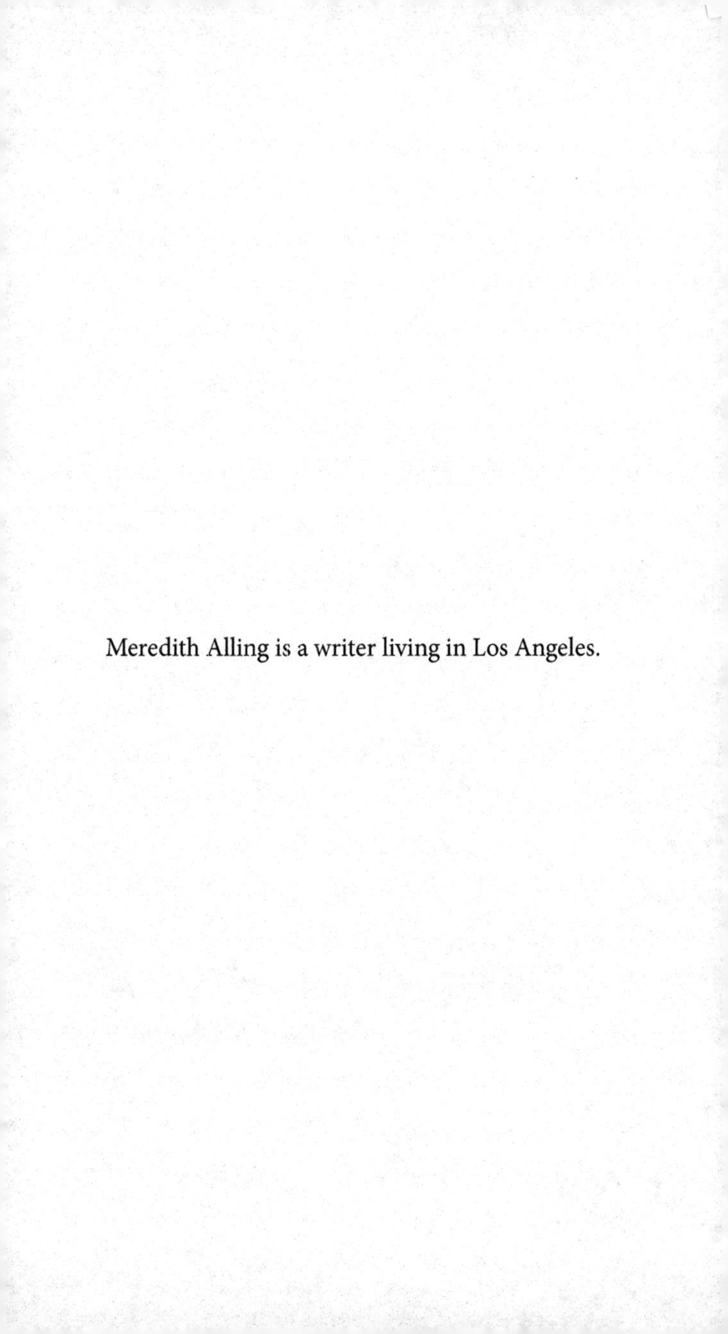
Meredith Alling is a writer living in Los Angeles.

CPSIA information can be obtained
at www.ICGtesting.com
Printed in the USA
FSOW04n1208091116
27112FS